MW01688496

Lion's Share

Lion's Share

Russ Lippitt

Ravenhawk™

Books

For the underground music scene; for the ‘greaser’ donning his black-leather jacket and high-cuffed blue jeans; for the ‘punk’ with the “fuck you” attitude sporting a green Mohawk; for the ‘boot and brace’ wearing ‘Skin.’ This book is dedicated to all of you.

Lion"s Share

RUSS LIPPITT

Ravenhawk™ Books

This is a work of fiction. All characters, events, places and reference materials portrayed in this novel are either fictitious or are used fictitiously. Any similarities to persons living or dead is purely coincidental and should not be inferred.

Lion's Share

Copyright © 2008 by "Russ Lippitt"

All Rights Reserved

Book Design by Shelly Geraci

Cover Art by Matt House

Author Photo courtesy of Dave Deluxe

Library of Congress Cataloguing-in-Publication Data
Lippitt, Russ -
Lion's Share / Lippitt, Russ - 1st ed. p.cm.

"A Ravenhawk™ Book"

ISBN 1-893660-15-X

I. Title

2007 LCCN

Printed in The United States of America

Prologue

"Greasers, punks, preps, beaners, niggers, chinks, ragheads, and crackers..." We humans seem to have an unquenchable penchant for hanging uncomplimentary jackets on each other. Why is that? Why do we continue to fear and condemn what we insist on not attempting to understand or tolerate? Deep down inside, we must all know that we are all more alike than we are different. Each one of us has a dark side. Each one of us has an heroic side. We are all capable; we are all failures.

This is the story of one of 'us.' A greaser, a punk, a criminal, perhaps, but nonetheless, a hero to a few. Someone looked up to for life's answers by a kid that perhaps believed he was nothing, had nothing, and would never be anything but a punk, a greaser.

This is the story of a greaser—My friend. Yes, I looked up to him, idolized him, wanted to be just like him, and regardless what you may think, he saved my life.

This is Billy's story.

"He said that there was one only good; namely, knowledge and one only evil, namely ignorance. He declared that he knew nothing, except the fact of his ignorance."
—Diogenes Laertus, Socrates, XIV-XVI

Chapter One

"First say to yourself what you would be; then do what you have to." —Epictetus, Chapter XXIII

THE ROOT OF ALL EVIL

"Billy! Hey, Billy!" Where are you? Hey, Billy!"

"Shut up, Hank! I'm over here in the bushes."

Hank walked quietly over to the shadowed bushes.

"What are we doing here, Billy?"

"What are you, stupid Hank? I told you last week at school why we are here. Now give me the stuff."

"What stuff?" Hank dug deep into his pockets. "Oh I forgot it."

"What?"

"Look Billy, I had a lot of homework to do and I didn't think you were serious about this."

"I swear Hank, you would forget your head if it wasn't connected to your neck. Okay we, as you and I, are going to break in old man Firgey's house because I heard he has a shit-load of alcohol in his cabinet."

"I don't know Billy, my mom said we should stay away from Mr. Firgey's house. She said he's crazy and besides it's dark and freezing out here. Let's go home."

Billy grabbed his friend's thick neck.

"For fuck sake Hank, are you going to listen to *mommy* your whole life? We are greasers! And almost sixteen years old now. We should do what we want, when we want. Ain't I right? Awe, Hank are you coming or you gonna stay here and act like a little pussy?"

Hank glanced down and then back at Billy.

"Alright, but if we get caught, the story is that you brain-washed me and I had no choice in the matter."

"Wow Hank, did you think of that one all by yourself? Now let's go, and keep quite."

Billy slinked up to the front sliding glass door. He peered in, but it was too dark to see anything clearly. He looked around, and saw a large brick. "I guess I've gotta do everything myself around here." He cocked his arm and took aim.

"Stop! What, are you crazy? That will make too much noise. Maybe we should use this," Hank pulled out his lock pick tool.

"You asshole, I knew you were just playing dumb with me," Billy said.

"I had you going there for a while buddy. You know I would never let you down," Hank assured him. "Now move over and let a professional go to work."

Five minutes passed and then the glass door slid open.

"I got it! I got it!"

"Good, now let's go, and be quiet! We don't want to wake that old bastard up."

The boys crept inside. They closed the door behind them. Their eyes had difficulty adjusting to the darkness. The house smelled old and musty. The old wooden floorboards moaned underneath them.

"Over here, I think."

"Billy, do you know where you are going?"

"Of course I do, and keep your voice down," Billy whispered.

They crept along. A bong echoed throughout the house.

Hank's mouth dropped open. Billy quickly grabbed him and shoved his hand over his friend's mouth.

"It was just the grandfather clock you idiot."

"I don't like this, let's get out of here," Hank whined.

"Would you stop being a scared-ee cat. We're almost there."

They crept along when a glimmer of something caught the corner of Billy's eye. Moonlight streamed through a crack in the roof, illuminating a silvery object.

"Look, Hank, over there."

"What is it?" Hank asked quietly.

"I don't know, but I'm gonna find out."

"No Billy, let's stick to the original plan."

Billy ignored Hank's suggestion and trekked over to the object. Hank drew a deep breath and then followed him.

Billy grabbed it, "It's some kinda handle," Billy opined.

Hank ripped the curious object away from him, "Yeah, and there's a button on it too." An apprehensive Hank pressed the button. A hidden four-inch blade zipped out.

"Woooooow!" they both exclaimed.

"It's a switch blade!" Billy caressed the slick blade of steel. "Cool!"

HEY! WHAT THE HELL ARE YOU KIDS DOING IN HERE?" A gruff voice bellowed.

They scattered toward the door, like roaches. Billy forgot that Hank had slid the door shut. A rotund Hank was right behind him. Billy slammed into the glass door. Hank pounded full throttle into Billy's back. The force of the impact sent Billy straight through the door. Shattered glass flew everywhere and they tumbled onto the lawn. Billy was up in a flash and ran down the road. A frightened and paralyzed Hank yelled, "Billy...don't leave me!"

Billy ran back to help his friend. The crotchety old man didn't have a prayer, he would not catch them. Their initial shock and surprise wore off as they laughed and raced off into the crisp night air. They ran for four blocks to an abandoned city park. It had been neglected for years, and was overgrown with tall weeds. A perfect place for the local teenagers to hide, and hang out.

They sat down at the graffiti-riddled picnic table.

"Billy! don't leave me!" Billy squawked, mocking Hank.

"Fuck you man! I almost shit my pants."

"Billy, Hank, come over here," called a distant voice.

"Who, Who's there?" Hank asked.

"Come out of from under there or I'm gonna kick your fucking ass!" Billy threatened.

The glow of a cigarette caught their attention as the scraggly kid emerged out of the shadows with his over-sized flannel jacket.

"Take a chill pill man, it's only me."

"Fuck Guy, you scared the shit out of us!" Billy said.

"You dudes up to no good again?" Guy asked.

"Yep, and where the hell were you?" Hank pulled a cigarette from behind his ear.

"I had another fight with my dad, and he kicked me out of the house again because he thinks I stole his coke."

"Well did you?" Billy asked.

"Hell yeah. But you are not supposed to accuse your only son."

"Do you still have it?" Billy asked with a big grin.

"What, do I look stupid? I snorted that shit right away before the old man got home from work."

"Man, you never save any of that stuff."

"Hey Guy, look what I stole from old man Firgey's house." Billy yanked the knife from Hank's back pocket. "It's a switch blade!"

"What do you mean Billy, 'look what I stole?' We both took it," Hank declared.

"I saw it and grabbed it first!"

"Yeah, but I pressed the button to figure out it was a knife," Hank said.

Billy stepped into Hank's face, "Oh yeah Hank, if you kept your fucking voice down we'd probably be in the house right now still taking shit!"

"Fuck off, if you stuck with the original plan we would be drinking some hard liquor right now!" Hank claimed.

They bickered back and forth until Guy stepped in between them, "Why don't you girls stop bitching and act like men and fight over it."

Billy glared at Hank, nodded and walked out into the street light. "Come on then, Hank!"

As he turned to face them, they saw blood drizzling down his face from a head wound.

"Come on, fuck!" Billy yelled, raising his hands tauntingly.

A nervous Hank announced, "I'm not going to fight you!"

Billy drew the switchblade out of his back pocket and tossed it down at Hank's feet, "Here, use the knife. You clearly have the advantage now, so come on!"

Hank crouched down and picked up the knife, peering at Billy. "I'm not going to fight you," Hank walked slowly back to the picnic table.

"Yeah, I was just kidding about the fighting thing," Guy said, realizing that Billy was too caught up in the moment.

"You stay out of this, Guy. This is between me and mama's boy!"

"What did you say?" Hank challenged.

"You heard me, is the little *mama's boy* gonna run away like his mom, who split from his dad?" accused Billy.

Hank sprang to his feet and confronted him.

"You take that back!" he shouted, pushing Billy.

"Why don't you make me, Hank!"

The boys stood face to face in the street light staring each other down. The tension between them thickened. Finally, Hank broke down and said, "Here! Take the fucking knife if you want it so bad!"

Billy put down his dukes and took the knife from Hank's hand all the while, grinning. It was the first time Guy and Hank had ever seen that particular grin and it wouldn't be the last time either. His nefarious, cocky and downright nasty look spoke volumes to them. They then sensed that something deep inside Billy was not normal.

They went back to the table and sat down. Billy broke the uneasy silence and told the story about their escapades at Firgey's house. The boys joked around with each other, having a good time.

He recalled Hank's panic and once again mocked him. "Don't leave me Billy!"

Hank was not amused.

Billy used the switchblade to carve his name into the wooden table.

Guy glimpsed a shadowy boyish figure approaching from across the street.

"Look everybody, here comes Angel," Guy sniffed in and rubbed his nose.

"Man, if Angel was my girlfriend I wouldn't leave the house. I'd be too busy fucking her," Hank grabbed his crotch lustfully.

"You wish Hank, everybody knows that she likes Billy here. And everybody knows that Billy is too stupid to see that!" Guy said.

"Would you two shut the fuck up. We are just good friends."

"What are you trouble-makers doing out here besides making a lot of noise? Don't you know tomorrow is a school day?" Angel removed her glasses and rubbed the bridge of her nose.

"Hey Angel, why don't you and I walk over to the bushes over there. I've got something I want to show you," Hank proposed.

"Um, no thanks Hank, anything you got to show me is most likely small and not worth it," Angel retorted.

Billy and Guy roared with laughter.

"Well, then, fuck you bitch!" Hank puffed up his stocky figure.

"Hey, don't talk to her like that, dickhead!" Billy ordered.

"Anyways, the reason I came out here is that my dad is trying to sleep. He told me to tell you guys to keep it down, especially you Hank."

"Oh wow, we should be quiet then because the dyke's dad said so," sneered Hank.

Billy glared at him. "What's wrong with you Hank? Show a little respect, asshole."

Hank's comment totally disgusted Angel.

"Um, Billy, would you come across the street and have a talk in private with me?" Angel asked.

"Yeah, sure Angel. I'll be right back and don't you fucks talk shit about me while I'm gone," Billy cautioned.

As Billy and Angel walked off, Hank yelled, "Yeah, you know that dude Billy, I heard he's a real jerk!"

"Yeah, yeah I heard that too!" Guy agreed.

Billy looked back at them and shook his head.

Angel grabbed his hand and pulled him across the street.

"Oh Billy, your blue eyes are so dreamy! You have the best hair ever!"

Angel and Billy ignored Hank's jabbing comment.

The street light, revealed the dried blood encrusted on his face. "Oh my God, Billy, you are bleeding!" She pulled some tissues from her pocket and gave them to him. He dabbed at the dried blood and then pressed the tissues into the oozing cut on his forehead.

"Why do you do this to yourself? And why the hell do you hang around with such assholes? You are better then that, and you know it."

He couldn't look her in the eye. "They are my friends and I always have good times with them."

Angel shook her head, "Billy...I got your homework for you from last week when you did not show up to class again. Ms. Cobb is worried that you are taking the wrong path through life. I'm worried too."

"Angel, how long have we known each other?"

"You know, we grew up together, so I would say all our lives."

"You always have good advice for me, but I know what I'm doing. Don't worry about me."

Angel managed half-a-smile, "I just can't figure you out.

When you do go to school, you get straight A's."

Still unable to look into her eyes, "I get bored at school too easily. I need things to keep me busy, like working on my bike."

Angel's sincere demeanor was marred by her frustration with his attitude. "I don't know how to help you, Billy."

"I didn't know I needed help. I'll be fine, you watch, old Billy boy will always come out on top."

"Hey Billy!" Yelled Pike, Angel's kid brother, hanging half-way out his bedroom window.

"Get back in bed, or I'll tell mom about your brass-knuckles!"

A reluctant Pike pulled himself back into his room.

"So, he likes them?"

"Yeah, thank you for that one, Billy."

"What?"

"Did you notice his hair?"

Billy smiled and nodded in approval, "It's a nice pompadour."

"He is starting more and more to look like you. You know he idolizes you, don't you?"

Billy chuckled.

"What the hell are you guys doing over there anyway?" Hank yelled.

Billy glanced at Hank and then redirected his attention on Angel.

"Look Angel, I'll try to make it to school tomorrow. Now will you just get off my back?" he pleaded.

"Well, I guess I'll see you tomorrow then," Angel said, as she watched him walk back into the scraggy park. She sighed deeply as she walked back to her house.

Billy plopped on the table and lit up a cigarette.

"Did you hold her hand?"

"Fuck you, Hank! She just had to get some things off her chest."

"By the looks of her chest, it seems like she got rid of those things a long time ago," Hank joked.

"Yeah, yeah, your just quite the fucking comedian aren't you?"

"Did you guys hear that a new kid moved into that house across the street from me?" asked Guy.

Billy and Hank glared at him.

"Yeah, I heard he has a bad reputation. Maybe he could hang out with us in The Click," Guy suggested.

"Really? What's his name?" Billy asked.

"Well, I heard his fucking mom yelling, 'Kelly would you stop doing that? Kelly would you act like a human being? Kelly, blah, blah, blah...' Quite frankly she's driving me fucking crazy!"

"Kelly, huh? Kind of a fruity name but he sounds like he's got potential. After school tomorrow, let's go and check out his house," Billy suggested.

"You going to school tomorrow, Billy?" asked Guy.

"Yes Guy, you got a problem with that?" an agitated Billy asked.

Guy could only manage a smirky look in the opposite direction.

"Alright fuckers, I'm going home. I'm starved," announced Billy.

"I guess I'll go home too," Hank yawned. "It's getting late."

"Gee thanks Hank, I guess I'll sleep here in the park with the fucking dogs," Guy said.

"I'm just fucking with you," Hank said with a grin. "Let's go back to my house and ask my mom if you can stay over for a week or two again until things cool down."

It was after midnight when Billy walked through the front door and found his mom waiting for him in the living room.

"And where were you young man?"

"Oh, you know, just cruising with the boys at the park."

His concerned mother replied, "Well I saved dinner for you. It's in the oven."

"Thanks Mom, I'm starved."

"I told your father that you were at Angel's house helping her study."

He gave her a big hug. "I don't know what I would do without you, Mom. I'm going to grab a bite to eat and then I'm going to sleep. I had a rough day today," he said as he walked into the kitchen.

"I know," she said.

He stopped and looked back at her, confusion blanketed his young face.

"We will talk about it tomorrow. And Billy, get a good night's sleep," she said with a smile.

He knew that look in her eyes. She knew what he did that night. It was her way of expressing disapproval. He would not sleep well that night. The last thing he wanted was for his mother to be disappointed, and think poorly of him.

***

That morning, one unoccupied seat remained in English class; next to Angel. Billy strolled into the classroom just as his name was called for attendance. All eyes were on him, a cigarette jammed over his right ear.

"Present!" Billy shouted piercing the quiet room.

"I'm glad you decided to join us this morning, Billy," Ms. Cobb stated.

"Well I'm glad to be invited to such a prestigious event," Billy quipped as he sat down at his desk. He leaned over and whispered to Angel, "What's up her ass?"

"It's just her way of showing that she cares. Did you do your homework, Billy?"

"No, I'll just do it in class."

"That is a complex and in-depth research paper that is due in about an hour!"

"You doubt my ability? Well, I've never!" he joked, "Just watch me." he then went to work on the paper.

Ms. Cobb began the morning's discussion on 'philosophical phraseology.' "Have any of you ever heard the idiom; phrase, if you will, 'lion's share' before?" Ms. Cobb asked, and then waited for a response. "Nobody? Okay, well, it means, 'the best or greatest part.' And as you should know, the king of the jungle is?"

Angel yelled out, "The lion!"

"That's right, Angel. In the animal kingdom, there exists a strict, natural code, a hierarchy. Animals live in a natural universal order, an evolutionary food chain, if you will. When you are on the lower end of the food chain, you are prey. But when you are on top, you are the predator, you rule. You get a bigger slice of the pie. So in jungle society, the lion, being *the king of beasts,* so-called, has most everything he desires. Hence, the idiom, 'lion's share!'"

Ms. Cobb continued her lecture. She also noticed that he was not paying attention to a word she said. He was obviously pre-occupied with something else. "Now who can tell me why this chain works the way it does? Billy?" Ms. Cobb barked.

Startled, he looked up from his writing and focused his eyes on his teacher. She snatched the cigarette from his ear.

"Huh? What was the question?"

His classmates watched the reparté intently.

"Billy, are you paying attention to today's lesson plan?" She asked as she circled his desk like a predatory shark poised to take a bite. "You know Billy, this philosophy, methodology, is important for you to grasp, learn, and retain. I mean, do you have any goals in life? Where do you see yourself in five years? How will you achieve your 'lion's share?'" Her tone seemed quite condescending to him.

He threw his pencil down on the desk.

"Put it this way, teach, far as goals, you don't need to know them. I see myself pissing off the world in five years. And I don't know anything about no 'lion's share.' Sounds like a Germs song to me."

Disgusted by his attitude, Ms. Cobb crumbled the cigarette. "You are supposed to be listening to me and not writing! Let's see what is so important that you could not wait to write." She grabbed the paper from his desk. "Billy...this is your essay that is supposed to be done by now!"

"Correct me if I'm wrong teach, but that paper is due at the end of the class."

"This assignment is a week's worth of homework. It cannot be researched without reference materials, or concentrated study, and then written in one hour."

"Obviously we are not seeing eye-to-eye here. A week, an hour, as long as it's done when that clock hits twelve noon. So who gives a flying fuck how long I worked on it?" Billy dug into his pocket and pulled out a five dollar bill and flung it at her. "Since that was my last cigarette, why don't you be a good girl and buy daddy a new pack?" he smirked.

"That's it mister! I've tried to help you, but you are just impossible. I want you to march straight to the principal's office, right now!"

As he leapt to his feet he ripped the essay from her hand, slammed it to the desk and wrote his name on it. He then glanced at Angel, conveying 'I tried.'

"Oh, Billy," murmured Angel.

He strutted toward the classroom door. "Oh yeah, teach, do you need anything from the store? Like a dildo, maybe, Mizz Cobbwebs?"

The students struggled not to smile or laugh.

Ms. Cobb seethed in anger.

Angel's heart sank in disappointment.

He pulled out another cigarette from the pack he had stuffed in his back pocket. Pushing people's buttons to the max jazzed him. He entered the hall restroom and found Hank, Guy and a new face, combing back his greasy slick hair. His beady eyes sized up Billy as he walked in.

"Hey, Billy, how's it hanging?" Hank asked.

Billy fired up his cigarette as he looked the kid up and down, "So who's that?"

"This is that guy we were telling you about. The one that moved in across the street from me. His name is Kelly, but he wants to be called Stick Boy."

"That is *Sick Boy* wisenheimer," Kelly replied.

Unimpressed, Billy took a long deep drag off his cigarette.

"Well Sick Boy, what do you do for kicks?"

"Anything you are up to."

Billy continued to size him up as he nodded. "Alright! I like your attitude, Sick Boy. Why don't we stir up a little trouble then?" Billy flicked his cigarette onto the tiled floor, and headed out.

Hank and Guy were not far behind him.

Sick Boy hesitated for a second and thought, *What did I get myself into?* He then ran after them. "Hey, wait up!"

Chapter 2

"Chaos often breeds life, when order breeds habit."
—Henry Brooks Adams (1838 - 1918)

LOVE... AND HATE

The four boys together just looked like trouble. The funny thing was, most of the time, they never went looking for trouble, it just had a way of finding them.

"Where are we going?" Hank asked.

"We are going to the park to chill for a while."

They walked down the sidewalk as if they owned it. Billy never walked on the sidewalk. He had this speech, on how, "Sidewalks are for mindless people who are doing what they are told." He would go on to say, "You are only walking on this side-walk because they told you to walk here and not there." He would point energetically from the sidewalk to a freshly cut lawn. "Fuck that! I walk where I want to!" So naturally one would see Billy, off walking on other people's lawns or sometimes even on the road, while everybody else stuck to the sidewalk.

They passed a neighborhood called, 'The Hills.' This neighborhood was where everyone lived the American dream. The big houses, perfect wives and kids, the white picket fence with a pedigree dog in the back yard.

Billy and The Click were certainly not welcome here. As

they passed the houses they could see the residents giving them disapproving or frightened looks. Billy over heard a woman saying, “Aren’t those boys supposed to be in school? Is that Billy? I feel sorry for his mother.” He never cared what people thought of him. In fact, he got off on the reputation he had for being a rebel.

They arrived at the park and saw six teenagers sitting at the graffiti marked table. The boys stopped, they eyed the unwelcome visitors and talked amongst themselves. When they were ready, they walked over to the invaders. Billy noticed the ‘Letterman’ jacket and a crew cut that only one asshole in town had, Bradley. He sat at the table with his preppie goons and some girl. It was a known fact that Bradley, or as The Click called him, ‘the Bradster,’ had all the muscle in town, so no one could fuck with him. He desperately hated Billy because of his fear that Billy had the potential of taking over the town. The kids in this town were split up into two groups; Billy’s and Bradley’s. You were with one, or the other. It was the classic battle of greasers vs. preps.

The boys stood behind Billy with their fists clenched, waiting for the first move.

“Hey there Billy boy, aren’t you supposed to be in school. I think you might be missing nap time,” Bradley quipped, delighted by his self-perceived cleverness.

He had heard what Bradley said, but his attention was somewhere else. The blonde bombshell who was sitting next to Bradley had caught Billy’s eye. He turned his head to look at Bradley and replied, “Where is your car, *Bradster*?” he then glanced down the street. “Did daddy take it away again because you missed the big pass at last nights football game?”

The girl giggled quietly.

Bradley whipped his head around and focused on her, “Shut up, bitch!” his hand threatened a swat.

She slowly put her head down. Billy looked at the girl, and then at Bradley, feigning disgust.

“What? Are you recruiting from the loony bin now?” Bradley peered in the direction of Sick Boy.

“Are you talking to me? I’ll fucking kill your poser ass!”

Sick Boy threatened, as he stepped toward Bradley.

Billy grabbed Sick Boy and looked into his eyes, "Let me handle this, alright?" He turned to face Bradley, "What the fuck do you want, Bradley?"

"Don't act stupid, you know why I'm down here in this shitty park, where you losers hang out. My uncle's house got broken into last night. The fuckers took a valuable knife. Would you know anything about that?"

He stared at Bradley full of hate.

"Hey, I'm talking to you, you piss-ant-nobody. I think you and your pussy friends did it, see. I'm gonna find out one way or another and when I do, all hell is going to break loose!" Bradley stood up and walked off. His goons followed right behind him.

The girl hesitated to move from the table, but she quickly changed her mind when Bradley yelled out, "Let's go doll, or I will not let you ride in the front seat of my car. She popped up and ran. She glanced at Billy as she ran by. He got a whiff of her perfume, he had never smelled anything so pure and beautiful before.

Bradley grabbed her long blonde hair and ripped down on it. He whispered something in her ear and then pulled her back into him, and off they went, back to The Hills.

Billy took a few steps toward them, he wanted to do something alright, but then he stopped and mumbled, "Yeah, that's right, all Hell *will* break loose."

"What a fucking asshole!" Sick Boy said.

"Yeah what a loser, that guy is like five years older than us. You would figure he has better things to do than being a prick all the time." Hank sat on the table.

"I don't get it, that girl was 'Monroe' hot. Why the fuck is she hanging around with an asshole like that?" Sick Boy shook his head.

Billy answered him, "He's got money. And I don't know much about girls, but I think they like assholes."

"Oh, then you should have three girlfriends, Billy!" Hank teased.

"You're so fucking funny, I forgot to laugh. I'm going home to work on my bike. I'll see you cats later." Billy walked home, flipping the knife open and then closed, over and over.

"He seems a little disturbed," Sick Boy noted.

"He has a rough family life. I guess that scene with Bradley, and that girl bothered him," Hank sensed Billy's sadness.

"What do you mean?"

"Well, his father used to beat him up on a regular basis. Billy got older, bigger, and started to fight back. One day his mom stepped in between them and his father beat on her. Billy blames himself on what's happening to his mom."

Hank and Guy continued to tell Sick Boy horrible stories about Billy's home life, as they watched him disappear in the distance.

Billy arrived home and opened the garage door to pull his motorcycle onto the driveway. He looked around for his tools but could not find them. He walked into the front door and yelled, "Honey, I'm home," mimicking Ricky Ricardo from "I Love Lucy." He did not receive a response. "Mom, where are you? Mom, have you seen my toolbox?" he scampered around the house, looking for his mother.

"Mom!...Mom!" He began to get concerned and went faster looking through all the rooms. "MOM!...MOM!"

"I'm in the bathroom, honey."

Relieved, he walked into the bathroom. She was bent over the sink, washing her face.

"You scared me for a second, Mom. For a while I thought..."

She looked up at her son, sullen, and beaten. She had two black eyes, cuts, and bruises all over her body. She began to cry.

He embraced her and held on to her tight. They slowly wilted to the floor. On their knees, he held her tighter and whispered, "It is getting worse, Mom. We've got to leave now!"

"I do...No I don't...Oh God, I don't know how to, Billy... We have no money, and we have no where else to go, all of my friends are your dad's friends really. Nobody will help us."

"I don't care Mom, this is not healthy. I'm sick and tired of his shit!"

"Billy, look at me, honey. I don't love your father any more. I just love you. And I'm afraid for you."

She saw the hatred in his eyes. "I see it in you, Billy."

"What do you see?" Billy asked curiously.

"Your father."

He stood up and raised his voice, "I am nothing like that asshole. That guy is a low life wife-beater who can't pay his bills on time. He drinks so much he could be a fucking fish! In fact, I don't remember the last time I've seen him. Oh that's right, I don't go by any 'bars' or 'jails,' so why would I see him? I am nothing like him, Mom!"

"You're not like him now, but your father started like this too. Not going to school, robbing people's homes, and staying up late. It leads to the same place— nowhere. I know you're smart, Billy. Don't be afraid to use what you've got upstairs."

He sat down on the toilet seat. "You know Mom, Angel has been telling me the same stuff, too."

"Well she seems to be a smart girl. Why don't you go out with her? She obviously likes you."

"What do you know about that?" he blushed.

"A mother knows all, my son," she hung the wet wash-cloth over the shower door.

He walked over to her, and gave her another hug.

"Don't become like you father. For God's sake. Please!"

He looked into her eyes and said, "How about this Mom, I'll be a good kid in school, at the park. Where ever. But you have to start looking for some kind of option to leave that jerk! I don't care how we do it, but it must be done. And, I'll see what I can do, too."

"Billy, please don't do anything stupid."

"Hey, you know me, I would never do anything stupid." He headed toward the door, "I'm not going out or anything, I'm just going to the store before it closes to buy some cigs. Are you going to be alright?"

"Yeah, yeah, I'll be fine honey, just hurry back, okay?"

"Billy! Billy!"

He galloped back into the house. "What? What's wrong?" he looked around frantically.

"Can you pick up a pack for me too?" his mother politely asked, handing him a five dollar bill.

"Sure, but this one's on me," he refused to take her money and walked out of the house. He actually did not leave to only get cigarettes, but to blow off some steam. Walking down the street he didn't say anything, but his mind raced, going a million miles per hour. *What am I gonna do? What should I do? How...am...I...going...to...do...it?* He stopped by the local convenience store, 'Sgt. Liquors.' He walked in and got a warm greeting from the clerk, Mickey.

"How things going, young Billy boy?"

"Not too good, Mickey," he shook his head.

"A kid like you should be having fun, man. Not thinking so much. What's so wrong that it's got you down, man?"

"You know Mick, same shit, different day. I need two packs of Lucky Strikes. One filter and the other of course, sweet non-filter."

"I'm assuming these are for your mother," Mickey said with a wink. "You know Billy, these things will kill you." Mickey grabbed the packs from behind the glass and handed them to him.

"Yeah, so will cholesterol, you fat bastard," Billy snorted, as he grabbed for his wallet. He looked in his wallet and realized he had spent his money on some video games in the arcade the other day.

"Um, Mickey, I'm kinda short today."

"Take the cigarette's and get out of here you little rascal." Mick reached over the counter and ruffled up his hair.

"Thanks Mick, I owe you one."

"Yeah, yeah, you can pay me back by pulling the plug when I'm on my deathbed!"

"Hey Billy! Don't worry, good things happen to good people."

The clerk's out-of-the-blue statement startled him as he

walked out the door. He thought, *Yeah right, Mickey, that's why my mom gets beat-up on a daily basis*. He opened the pack of cigarettes and still felt distraught about everything that had happened in his life. He walked to the park to sit, and think. He dug in his pocket for a light. "Fuck, I forgot my matches at home!" He put his head down and placed his hands on top of his head. *Can anything else bad happen?* A click disturbed his thoughts.

"Is this what you are looking for?" the sweet voice asked.

He looked up slowly. He first saw a gorgeous pair of legs. His eyes continued up, surveying the rest of the lovely body. *A decent rack too.* He gazed into her face. What a shock! The girl who was with Bradley and his goons earlier, holding out a Zippo. He stuttered, "Oh yeah, thanks," he took the Zippo and lit his cigarette.

"Do you have an extra one of those for me?"

"Yeah, sure, here you go," he gave her a cigarette and lit it up for her. The Zippo had a Lucky Strike logo.

"This is a bad-ass Zippo you got here," he said, while rubbing and examining the lighter in his hands.

"Thanks, I really don't smoke, but I like this lighter."

He smiled sheepishly at her.

"It's Billy, right?"

"Yep, Billy's the name and pissing off the Bradster, is the game."

She laughed, "You're a funny guy, Billy...and cute too."

He looked around and pointed at himself, "Who me? Well, I mean, I try my best."

She giggled some more. They sat quietly for a few moments.

"So what's *your* name?"

She looked up at him and batted her eyelashes, "Savanna."

The way she said her name made him just melt.

"Wow, Savanna, That's the prettiest name I ever heard."

She blushed while he continued to examine her luscious curves.

"I know I don't know you, Savanna, but I need to ask you

this."

She looked really puzzled.

"You are a very beautiful girl. You could probably get any guy you want. So why the fuck do you hang with that cocksucker Bradley?"

She took a few seconds to think before giving her answer. "Well Billy, let me tell you a little story about my life. I was born and raised in The Hills, and so was Bradley. My family has known Bradley and his family for a long time now. They all expect us to get married, have kids, the whole nine yards."

He shuttered at the idea. "Well Savanna, your family does not know him that well, I mean he treats you like shit."

She rebutted quickly, "Oh, no he doesn't! He gets mad sometimes, but he says he's sorry. He also buys me gifts all the time, so I know he loves me."

"Is that what love is? Buy you things, with the occasional abuse, Savanna? Shit, I hope I never fall in love then."

"Also, it is what my parents want. I know I will have a good life with him if I can just hang in there," Savanna took a deep drag of her cigarette.

"What? I...this...I'm at a loss for words here. 'If I can hang in there?' What a load of shit. Listen to me, this shit does not get better. It gets worse. I'm a product of it. My mom thought like you once, a long time ago. And now look at her, I mean I love her to death, but her life is over. She's got a deadbeat husband that beats up on her, she's got no job, all of her dreams went up in smoke when she said, 'I do.' She sits around the house all day getting fat. I ain't no picnic neither. I know I'm a fucked-up kid. I don't know who's to blame, but I can tell you my family doesn't help in the matter."

"No, no, he's not like that. He is usually nice to me, but just sometimes he loses his temper. I know he doesn't mean it, because he always apologizes to me later."

"You gonna keep telling yourself that? Are you in some kind of denial? I saw what I saw. He does not respect you."

Savanna's nose flared. She looked deep into his eyes, "What would you know about it anyway? You don't know me!"

Her eyes swelled with tears.

"I'm sorry, you're right, I don't know you, Savanna. In fact, I don't know why I'm telling you this. I guess I see something else in your pretty blue eyes. The last thing I wanted to do was make you cry. I'm sorry."

They sat quietly for a few minutes, staring off into the distance.

"I'm sorry too. I didn't mean to yell at you. I know that you were just trying to help me. Yeah, I guess rich girls like me got problems too."

"Yeah, I mean you are, what, fifteen, maybe sixteen, you should not be thinking of things like pleasing your parents and marriage. Fuck, you don't even look good with that guy." He circled around, and over her shoulder he whispered like the Devil in her ear, "You are a pretty girl and Bradley is an ugly son-of-a-bitch! You should be having fun, and not just legal fun."

"Yeah, you are right," she coyly looked over her shoulder.

"Of course I'm right, I'm always right."

She smiled and wiped the tears from her face.

He walked in front of her. "I'm curious, what kind of guys are you into?"

"Well I don't know. I like an educated boy with strong goals in life, I guess."

"Alright, anyways, fuck that! What kind of music do you like? What style are you into? What do you do for kicks?"

She looked at him with a smile and said, "Well Bradley likes—"

"No! Not what Bradley likes! What do *you* really like?"

"Well sometimes when I'm home alone, I go up to the attic and listen to my parents old records and dress up in my mom's old clothes. I do love the 50's look, but Bradley would never let me wear those clothes. He likes me wearing skimpy things that show off my 'good stuff.'" Savanna put up her fingers and gestured quotation marks, as she pushed out her breasts.

He took a hit from his cigarette and choked on it. "And what about for kicks?" He asked still choking on the cigarette smoke.

"Oh, I don't know," she thought for a moment and then replied, "Oh, I like to drink!"

He smiled, "Now you're talking. I got an idea, have you ever been to The Outsiders?"

"Um, no. Isn't that a greaser bar?"

"Hell yeah it is! It gets so rowdy, even the cops leave it alone. So you can do what ever you want."

"Yeah, Bradley would never take me to a place like that."

"That's why I'm takin' you. I know the bartender and he always lets The Click in. This Friday night a band called, 'The Blazing Hellcats' are playing. They are a cross between Rockabilly and Punk. I think you might like it. Would you like to go with me?" he asked with puppy-dog eyes.

"Okay...sure...it sounds like fun."

"The show starts at nine o'clock. So, I'll pick you up at ten."

She smiled and sauntered off, then she stopped and turned around. "Billy! Do you have a few cigarettes I can have?"

"Yeah, sure!" He reached in his jacket pocket and pulled out the unopened pack and gave it to her.

"Wow, thanks. I'll see you Friday, Billy," She pranced off toward her home in The Hills.

He waited until she had disappeared from sight, and then shouted, "FUUUUUUCK YEAAAAAH!!"

It started to get dark and he thought to himself, *Shit, tomorrow is Friday. I better get home and work on my bike.* He strutted down the street with a big smile on his face.

He arrived at his house and danced through the front door. He went into his mom's room where she slept peacefully. He reached in his black-leather jacket pocket to pull out the cigarettes. "What the fuck?" He then realized that he accidently gave his mom's pack to Savanna. He took his open pack and placed it on top of the dresser chest for her, then he left for the garage to search for his toolbox, he closed her bedroom door behind him.

"What an idiot I am! I can't believe I gave that pack away so easily. It totally slipped my mind," he spied the toolbox under a pile of dirty rags.

An hour had passed while he endulged himself, working on his motorcycle.

"Eh hem, eh hem!"

He looked up and Angel was hovering over him.

"Hey Angel, what's going on?" he continued to work on his bike.

She threw some papers down next to him.

He stopped working and looked at them.

"It's your essay that you turned into Ms. Cobb. Billy, you got a B+ and you didn't even try!" She yelled in a frustrated tone.

"Well that fucking sucks, I should have gotten an 'A'."

Angel looked at him like he was crazy, "Are you kidding? I worked on my essay for three hours, every day of the week and all I got was a C!"

"Well maybe you shouldn't work so hard next time, huh?"

Angel stared at him, baffled, and ready to strangle him. Instead, she turned around and stomped off mumbling, "Unbelievable, just unbelievable."

"Hey, Angel come back here, I was just kidding with you!"

She begrudgingly walked back to him, head down. "I'm sorry Billy, I just don't get you sometimes. You try so little at things, and they just naturally come to you. It's like you're really lucky."

"Trust me Angel, it's hard luck. I get burnt more than you think."

"I don't believe you," she looked up at him with a half-assed smile. "So, you are working on your bike again. Do you have it running yet?"

"It always ran Angel, I'm just tweaking and customizing her. Here, look at the speedometer," he pointed out that it read 140 miles per hour.

"I don't get it. What about it?"

"What! What do you mean, 'what about it?' This baby can run up to one hundred and forty miles per hour now. You know what that means, right?"

She paused for a few moments, consternation riddled her young features.

"Shit Angel, I can now hit 138 mph! Like the song, by The Misfits!"

She still stood there with a confused look.

He shook his head in disbelief. "Anyway, 138 is important to me, and at that speed...it's going to be fucking insane. I get a hard-on just thinking about it," he continued to wipe down his bike.

Angel shrugged her shoulder and said, "Okay."

"Well, that's something I appreciate," he grabbed a wrench and began to tighten a bolt. "Oh yeah! Guess who I am going out with this Friday night."

"I don't know, Bride of Frankenstein? The Devil?" she raised an eyebrow.

"Ha, ha, that's pretty funny. No. I'm going with Savanna to The Outsiders to see 'The Blazing Hellcats!'"

"Savanna? You mean that rich, high-maintenance girl that lives in The Hills and just so happens to be going out with the 'Bradster'."

He smiled and with his infamous cocky attitude, "Yep!"

"Okay, how did this happen?"

"I don't know. I just started to talk to her and we kind of hit-it-off."

"You don't have anything in common with her. What are you thinking?" Angel asked with tightly crossed arms.

"For your information, Angel she may be different from me but, she enjoys some of the same stuff I do. She's a nice person, I felt something I've never felt before."

"Billy, I know you. When you say she's a nice person, you really mean she has huge tits."

He laughed, "I admit, she does have a great body that takes my breath away. But I think we would have a good time together."

Shaking her head in disapproval, she asked, "And what will Bradley think of this?"

"Fuck the Bradster! He treats her like shit and she deserves better!"

"Oh, I see, and you can give her better."

He looked at her bewildered, "What do you mean by that?"

"I'm just saying, look at you. You're covered in oil from working on your motorcycle, and she probably thinks oil fuels a car. You're just two different people."

He turned away ignoring her and continued to work on the bike.

"I don't know...I think you'll just get hurt on this one. It won't be something that you can just walk away from, or in your case, *ride* away from."

"Don't worry about me Angel, I'll be fine. I know what I'm doing!"

She looked at him and sighed. "Well good luck then. Call me later and tell me what happened." She strolled off down the road back home.

He had always took Angel's advice to heart in the past, but this time, he was not listening. There was only one thing on his mind, Savanna. He picked up a rag and started to polish his motorcycle. "That's right baby, you, me, and Savanna are going out tomorrow. Gotta make you look good so she falls in love with you, like I am."

Anything for you, Billy.

He always had conversations with his motorcycle, as if it could talk back to him. At first, everyone thought he was nuts. But soon, people came to except it. He really loved his bike. He would rather die, then drive anything else. He once elaborated on a few reasons why his bike was better than any girl. "First, a bike always keeps you warm at night." He would continue with, "As long as you take good care of her, she will always love you." Finally, "She will always let you ride her." For Christ's sake, he named the damn thing. He never revealed the name of that bike. It was his first love.

He finished up on the motorcycle as a car drove up in the driveway, the horn blared at him.

The driver yelled out in a slur, “Mooove tha-at piece of shi-it out of the way!”

He glanced up, his father’s headlights shined bright in his face. He grabbed a rag from the ground and wiped off his hands.

“Boy, when I tell you t’do something, you bet...do it!”

Billy stared at him, as he kicked up the stand and pushed the bike onto the lawn. His father pulled into the driveway running over the tools left on the ground. He watched, filled with rage. Beer bottles fell out of the car as soon as his dad stumbled out. As he staggered past his son, Billy smelled the nauseating odor of puke, smoke, and stale beer, all mixed together.

“What you look at boy?” he squinted and rocked forward, attempting to focus his eyes on him.

“Nothing much. Nothing much at all!”

His dad stopped fumbling with his keys, “Well, well, well, little Billy bo-oy hads his mudher’s sm-mart-ass mouth.”

He jumped into his father’s face, unable to control the mounting rage. He examined the pathetic excuse for a man, “I don’t want to get into this again, *old man*,” he then leapt on his bike and kick-started it. He revved the engine over and over again.

“Oo-oh, I so-o scared, you look so-o tough’n that motor...cycle.”

“You’re a fucking asshole! You know that? One day it’s all gonna come back and slug you in the face! You’ll never even know what hits you!”

The drunken sperm-donor stumbled toward him with his fists clenched, “You threat’n me boy?”

He revved up Jean’s engine so he could not hear his father. He then peeled out of the driveway. The unsteady lush chased after him for only a few yards before becoming to winded to continue, he picked up a wrench and threw it at his son.

Billy turned and flipped him off, then ripped down the road. He headed up to Dead Man’s Curve. It was called that because it was death’s last stop; a two mile stretch, with a steady incline to nowhere. A five hundred foot drop. He drove the back roads, and pulled up to the beginning of the steep winding hill.

He red-lined the engine, and peeled out, yanking the accelerator grip back. He jam-shifted into 2nd gear. At sixty miles per hour, he shifted to third and hit one hundred and five miles per hour in eleven seconds. He put his head down, the wind in his face became over-powering, making it difficult to breathe. Fourth gear! Then he jammed it into fifth. He was at 120, 122, 128 miles per hour. The bike began to vibrate. He looked down at the speedometer, *We're almost there!* He saw the lights from the town, as he climbed higher and higher. He knew that the road was coming to the end, but he did not care. His concentration remained locked on the road. The yellow stripes passed by so fast, it hypnotized him. He ground his teeth and gripped the handlebars. He was not afraid to die. Just then an image flashed across his mind that made him think twice. First, he saw his mom crying and looking down into a graveyard and then a second image, of himself, and Savanna holding hands somewhere. He did not recognize the place, but he envisioned the both of them smiling at each other.

I'm happy? He quickly shifted down two gears. *Oh shit, it might be too late!* Down to 70, 40, and then 20 miles per hour. The cliff's edge was in view. He turned the bike sharply to the left, sliding toward the end. A couple of rocks fell over the edge as he stared down from the precipice and into the abyss.

He engaged the kickstand and took out a cigarette. He looked out at the town's lights and pondered what the images that they caused his mind to form meant. He understood the first one, his mom would be devastated and the last thing he wanted to do was have her suffer anymore than she already had. Yet, the Savanna image puzzled and intrigued him at the same time. He then wiped the road debris off his bike with a polishing cloth that he kept under the seat.

"What's with that Savanna girl? I just met her, but I feel that I've known her my whole life. I feel close to her."

You're in love.

"...No, no, no. I'm not, Jean."

He shook his head, as he talked to his beloved bike.

Just a second ago, you were going to take us over the

edge. But then that image pops up, and you stopped...

"I don't know, baby. When I first saw her, I knew I would hook-up with her. I just could not take my eyes off of her. There is...something about her..."

Maybe you are growing up, maybe it is time to love someone else besides me. Besides, I'm just an engineered pile of nuts and bolts anyway.

"I guess we will find out tomorrow if she digs on me like I do on her."

CHAPTER 3

"And that one hunting, which the Devil designed for one fair female, lost him half the kind."
—John Dryden, 'The Theodore and Honoria,' line 227

The Big Night

Billy decided to stay at Dead Man's Curve that night. He leaned back on his bike and gazed at the stars. A full moon peeked over the mountain ridges. The wind began to pick up and he zipped his black leather jacket to keep warm. He laid down on top of his bike and slowly fell asleep.

He never dreamt much. His life was a living nightmare. Yet that night the most bazaar dream came to him. He could fly, and he was flying over places he had never seen before. The dream took him to an old looking castle. In front of it, a white horse stood with a silver-plated knight kneeling by it's side. He heard a woman's scream coming from the window of the story book castle. The knight had tears in his eyes. He wanted to get a closer look, however he was not in control of his flight.

He then came across an isolated, desert town. Billy looked down and saw people crowding around what looked like the gallows. He heard the crowd yelling, "He is just a boy, let him go! He has done nothing wrong. Love is not a crime."

He tried to look at the prisoner, but could not see who it was. The guards who were escorting him were twice as big as the boy. Billy again wanted to stay, but he was being dragged across the sky.

The third scenario he came upon was a jungle. All he could hear and see were explosions, yelling, and death. Some sort of war was taking place. Suddenly, he could no longer maintain his free-flight. He descended out-of-control through the trees. He fell hard into a heap of singed bushes. He stood up cautiously and heard bullets and bombs coming closer to him. Ahead, a soldier held a girl in his lap. He wanted to get a closer look, so he snuck through the bushes. The noise of the war suddenly started to fade as he drew closer to the couple. The soldier sat crying, holding a dead Vietnamese girl. Then the soldier looked up and yelled, "WHY! WHY!" He stood up with the limp body in his arms and gave her one last hug. Billy moved forward and stepped on a twig. The soldier looked up at him. His forlorn eyes expressed loss and emptiness as they gazed at one another.

"That soldier looks like me!" Startled, the soldier turned around and ran off into the bushes with the lifeless body. Billy fell to his knees. He closed his eyes, holding his head, shaking in disbelief. He opened his eyes and looked up, everything had turned black except for a pinpoint light in the distance. He stood up and walked toward it. As he edged closer he noticed that it was not a light, but a mysterious, shiny object on the ground. The closer he got, the more unbearable the object became to look at.

He Stretched out with one arm, and covered his eyes with the other. He strained for the object. Struggling to grip it, he latched on to it, closing his hand around it. The throbbing shine stopped. He opened his hand. A bright flash smothered his face. He re-gripped the hard object. He then opened his eyes; a flashlight!

"Hey boy, what are you doing up here?" the police officer peered over him.

Billy sat up on his motorcycle and wiped his eyes.

"Um...I don't know...I guess, I fell asleep."

"Yeah, well it's almost sunrise. I'm sure your parents are worried about you. Are you alright?"

"Yeah, I'm fine, I just had ah, um..." he looked down at his hand and then opened it. He was holding Savanna's 'Lucky Strike' Zippo.

"You should get home, son. In a few hours you should be in school."

"Yeah, yeah no problem. Just let me wake up a little and then I'll ride home."

The cop nodded and walked back to his patrol car. "Unit Thirteen, ten-twenty-two, Dead Man's Curve. Code four. Nothing happening up here, just a kid that I told to go home. Unit Thirteen, ten-eight."

"Unit Thirteen...copy traffic..."

"Ten-four," the officer sped off.

Billy looked at the Zippo, "What does this mean? Was that my past lives? Is this fate?" He waited a few minutes so the cop had a good head start. He did not want to run into him again. That cop was nice to him for only one reason, he did not know him and was probably new to the force. Usually cops and Billy bumped heads.

"Well, I better get home. Tonight will be my last chance to have fun. Then after that, a new life, a fresh start. I promise." Billy started his bike and rode home. It was around six thirty in the morning when he snuck in the house and quietly poured himself a bowl of cereal. His mother woke up and walked to the kitchen.

"Where did you go last night? Billy, you promised!"

"It's alright, Mom. I came back home but you were sleeping and I didn't want to wake you up. I went to work on my bike, but dad came home, and was being a real dick. So I went to blow off some steam and think about things. I'm still going to school, don't worry."

"Alright Billy, I am just so worried about you," she went over to the cabinet and took out a frying pan.

"You should have a good breakfast before going to school."

He glanced at the wall clock.

"No, that's alright Mom, you go back to sleep. This cereal will hold me over."

She wiped her eyes, sighed, and headed back to her bedroom.

"Oh Mom! I got some other good news... I met a girl and she is great. I'll tell you all about it when I get home from school."

She felt the happiness in his eyes and heart; it made her smile.

He heard two voices coming from the master bedroom. His father, now sober, came into the kitchen.

"How you doing there, Billy?"

He continued to munch his cereal and did not respond.

"Look, I'm sorry about what happened yesterday. I apologized to your mother and now I'm saying sorry to you. I hope you can forgive me, just like your mother has."

He stood up and walked out the door, "Yeah, well, I better get going to school before I'm late." He decided to walk to school instead of riding. He wanted so bad to forgive his dad, but he had heard that song and dance before and it had worn thin. He was tired of it and 'I'm sorry' did not cut it anymore.

He arrived at school ten minutes early. He walked to Ms. Cobb's classroom and took his seat. No one else had arrived in the classroom yet, but Billy sat there and did not say a word. He made some quick eye contact with Ms. Cobb, but she looked away quickly. They both sat there as a quiet tension filled the room. Finally, he stood up and approached her.

"I'm sorry Ms. Cobb, the way I acted yesterday. I just got a lot on my mind and I want to be good from now on. I know you've only been trying to help me, but I've been pushing you away. I'm sorry."

His words were a shock to her ears. "Well, Billy I am not going to give you any special treatment, no favors."

"That is not what I want, ma'am. I just want a chance to improve myself and my grades, that's all."

"Good to hear that, son. Now, please take your seat, class will be starting soon," Ms. Cobb continued to grade some papers.

As he sat down, the school bell rang. All of the students

rushed in and glared at him as they took their seats. Angel too, was surprised to see him in class two days in a row.

"Billy, what...what are you doing here?"

"What Angel, I can't come to my classroom?"

"Yeah, it is great to see you here, but I thought you were probably kicked out of school by now."

"No, I had a little talk with Ms. Cobb and everything is cool. Besides, I made a promise to my mom and also, Savanna likes guys with goals. I've got a goal now."

"What's the catch Billy? You doing this for a girl? You're so unpredictable."

"Unpredictable! Huh, that is a big word for you, Angel," he smiled.

"Well, I see you haven't lost your smart-ass attitude."

For the rest of that day he answered all questions thrown at him. He behaved as if he had become a model student. Billy possessed superior intelligence, but chose not to engage it most of the time, at least, not out in the open. Angel was so proud of him that day, she beamed as she listened to him answer every question with preciseness, confidence, and poise. The end of the school day came and the final bell rang. He had treated all of his teachers with a new found respect that befuddled some of them, and the rest of them were sure he was plotting something shocking or evil.

He walked down the hallway and stopped at the entrance to the boy's restroom. He hesitated for a second and thought. *Fuck it, they are still my friends.* He opened the door and to his surprise, instead of seeing The Click, he saw Bradley and his hench men.

"Well look-ee what we got here. If it isn't little Billy-Boy at school. Are we learning alot today?"

His stomach churned. "Fuck off Bradster, I can't be bothered with you today," he walked over to the mirror and washed his face. Bradley swaggered over to him and stood behind him, looking at him in the mirror.

"How many times have I told you not to call me Bradster?"

Billy looked at him through the mirror, “I don’t know and quite frankly I don’t give a flying fuck!”

Bradley grabbed him by the collar, and turned him around. “I’m going to beat the shit out of you one day, and you won’t have that smirk anymore!”

He wanted so bad to pull out his knife and shut that son-of-a-bitch’s mouth once and for all, but he was sticking to his promise. In a calm voice he said, “Are you done yet? Because I have something more important to attend to,” he pushed Bradley away.

“What? You have a hot date or something? Probably just one of your sluts that you hang around with,” Bradley and his goons laughed.

Billy cracked a grin, “Actually I do have a hot date tonight.” He walked out of the bathroom knowing that he would get the last laugh.

On his way home, he noticed a group of preps pushing around a little greaser kid. Billy lit up a cigarette and walked over to the scuffle to investigate. It was Pike being bullied.

“Hey kid, don’t you know being a greaser gets you beat up?” One of the prep boys pushed Pike to the ground, while his glasses flew off. The prep bully then stepped on Pike’s glasses and crushed them.

Billy strolled up to them cool and calm, “How’s it going guys? What’s the matter, couldn’t find something homoerotic to do, besides pushing a little kid around?” he took a hit off his cigarette.

“Stay out of this Billy, this is none of your business!”

“That kid has grease in his hair, and that’s all of my business.”

The preps intensified their attention on him and forgot about Pike.

“I know you don’t go to school Billy, but I figured at least you could count.” The lead prep said, as the rest of his crew clenched their fists.

He may have been out-numbered, but not out-classed. He took out his switchblade and flipped it open. The preps took a step back.

"I can count...all six of you, and I'll tell you all this...the first one that steps toward me, or the kid, dies!"

The preps looked at one another and decided to back off, a full retreat, this time.

"You're lucky this time, Billy! You too, kid! Real lucky!"

He stashed his persuader away and helped Pike off the ground.

"Yeah, real lucky," he laughed inside himself.

"Wow, Billy that's bad-ass."

"What are you doing, walking around by yourself out here?"

"I can take care of myself," Pike insisted, while he brushed the dirt off his shirt.

Billy laughed, "Yeah, before I came you really had them on the run."

Pike smiled and bent over to pick up his crushed glasses. "Shit! My Dad's gonna kill me."

"It's alright, you're better off without glasses. You look cooler without them." He smiled and flipped up his leather jacket collar. Billy took a drag of his cigarette, then gave it to Pike and walked off.

Pike watched him stroll down the street toward home. He then took a drag off the cigarette, and gagged.

As he approached the Park, he saw the boys at their table. He stopped by to see what they were up to.

"Hey fuck nuts, what's happening?"

"Oh nothing, Billy," Hank replied while Guy and Sick Boy joked quietly.

Bewildered, Billy asked, "What's so funny?"

"Oh, nothing. Sick Boy just told us a dirty joke," Guy laughed.

He suspected something fishy was going on and pushed them further to let him in on the joke. "Okay cock suckers, what's so funny?"

"Oh nothing at all, *teacher's pet!*"

The boys laughed out loud as they all pointed at him.

"Angel told us about it during lunch. She said that you changed and you will not be hanging out with such losers like us anymore," Hank said, unable to control his laughter.

"Fuck you guys, yeah, so what? I paid a little attention today at school. Maybe sometime you should too, so you won't be so fucking stupid, Hank!"

Hank blurted through laughter, "Yeah, and the best part is when she said, that you are doing all this for a *girl*!"

The boys rollicked heartily.

Billy could not do anything but grin and laugh too.

"Wow, that Angel has some crazy ideas sometimes," Billy looked away. Slowly the laughter died down.

"Anyway Billy, are you going to see that band tonight at The Outsiders?" Hank asked.

He wanted to say no. He knew now if he showed up with Savanna, they would all know what Angel said was true. So he blurted out the first thing that came to his mind. "Yeah, I'm going, but tonight we are going to play a game."

"Yeah, what's that?" Hank asked.

"Um...tonight is beaver hunting. So you fuck-ups, look your best...I want to see all of us greased-out and pomped high. The one that meets the hottest chick gets a free six-pack from each of us. Deal?"

"Okay!"

"Sounds like fun!"

"Yeah, sure, whatever."

Billy then looked at Sick Boy intensely, "and tonight, Sick Boy, is *your* initiation ceremony into The Click."

Sick Boy grinned, "It's about fucking time!"

"Cool, I'll see you sissies tonight then," he then walked home.

"So Hank what do I have to do? Beat somebody up? Rape a dog, chicken, what?"

Hank stared at Sick Boy and then put his arm around him.

"You have to drink."

"You're kidding, right? That's it? I fucking drink all the time!"

"No, this is a special drink. K-T-F-O."

Guy remained silent, smoked his cigarette and just shook his head.

Sick Boy scoffed at the idea, *A drink? A just a drink? I ain't afraid of that! Panzy-assed motherfuckers!* "Ok, bring it on whatever it is. UFO, CIA, KGB."

Billy turned the corner close to his house and started to think, it appeared perfect on paper. He would go out with Savanna, a girl he cared about. He would piss off Bradley, always a plus, getting under the Bradster's skin. And to top it all off, an easy win with the bet he made with the boys. The only tricky part was not to be seen with her walking in the door. It had to look like they met there.

He arrived home and went straight to his room, and collapsed onto his bed.

His mother knocked on the door as she walked into his sanctuary.

"Rough day at school, son?"

"Yeah Mom, I have to get used to this using my brain thing again."

"I know, Angel called me earlier and told me how you were so smart today."

"Jesus, man, she's been telling everybody. She's going to ruin my reputation."

"I think she likes you."

"No Mom, we are just good friends."

"I don't know Billy, she also told me about some girl you met and warned me to look out for you. She does sound concerned, and perhaps she is a bit jealous."

He fell back on his pillow, "Ahhh Savanna."

"Savanna?"

"I met her once, but when I first saw her I felt...fuzzy. Do you know that feeling, Mom?"

She rolled her eyes. "Once, a long time ago, but I was young and I didn't know what I wanted. I made a terrible mistake by letting him go. I made a bigger mistake thinking I was in love with your father and marrying him. Every bad has something good come out of it though," she winked at him.

"Wow Mom, I almost got misty-eyed there," he chuckled.

"Yeah, even though you are a smart-ass, I still love you," she beamed a smile and walked out of his bedroom.

He stood up and closed his bedroom door, then set his alarm clock. He ran and jumped on his bed and quickly fell asleep. He did not dream again as pitch-black filled his mind.

He woke to the annoying sound of the alarm clock. He rolled over and slammed the snooze button. Five minutes later, the alarm went off again. He grabbed the clock and threw it across the room. Slowly, he tried to get up, but fell back into bed. The phone rang a half an hour later. He jerked himself out of a dead sleep and answered the phone.

"Yeah, what?"

"Hey Billy, what the hell are you still doing there? You didn't fall to sleep again, did you?"

"What, what time is it? Where the hell is my alarm clock?" He looked around the room, dazed and confused.

"Dude, it's nine forty. The Blazing Hellcats are coming on soon. The first couple of bands have already played. Guy brang some coke and I don't want to brag, but I might have won the bet, I got a cutie's number."

"Really? Where's, Sick Boy?"

"I don't know. I think he's fighting outside. Some guy was talking shit to him earlier."

"Fuck, I'm missing all the fun!"

"Damn Skippy, you are. Hurry up!"

Billy slammed the phone down and ran to the bathroom. He grabbed his grease and pomped his hair. Then he raced to his closet and grabbed his leather. He went back into the bathroom and looked into the mirror. He smirked at himself and lit up a cigarette. "I like it!" he said in self-admiration. He ran to the garage and got on his motorcycle. He kicked the starter and rode off to Savanna's house.

As he pulled up to the majestic white house with a pretty little garden and perfectly manicured lawn, he gunned the engine a few times, until the porch light turned on. He waited impatiently, checking out the neighborhood. He noticed the people in the surrounding homes pulling back their curtains to get a quick look at the disturbance in their neighborhood. He just smiled and smoked his cigarette. Savanna came running out and boy, did she look good. She was wearing a red, fifty's style dress that resembled something that Betty Grable might wear. He threw her a helmet.

"So, are you ready to have some fun?"

"I'm kinda scared, I've never been on the back of a motorcycle before. Where is *your* helmet?"

"I don't wear a helmet, it messes up my hair. Don't worry, me and Jean will take care of you."

She strapped on the helmet, "Okay, um, who's Jean?"

He blushed, turned his head, "Oh, it's just my bike's name."

He put his head down in shame because nobody knew the name of that bike until now. He revved the engine a few more times. Savanna's parents peered out the window.

"Hurry let's go. My mom and dad are watching!"

"Alright, you're the boss," he grinned and peeled out, popping a wheely down the street, they sped down the road. He knew that the band was going to start soon. He pushed the bike past one hundred miles per hour and Savanna squeezed his waist tighter.

"Billy, you are going too fast, please slow down!"

He heard her but he kept going faster, laughing.

"Billy, slow down! Billy!" she yelled.

Faster and faster they went.

Her arms, wrapped tight around him, her grip began to cut off his circulation. The faster he went the tighter her grip became.

She screamed louder and louder, pleading with him. "Billy! Billy!...This is...Great! W-o-o-o-w!"

He knew she was having fun, although fear pumped adrenaline all throughout her vivacious body.

He ran red lights and cut off cars. He challenged every vehicle on the road.

"YEE! HEE! YEE-OW!" he cried.

She hit him in the back of the head, "Okay Billy, you can slow down now."

He had had his fun and started to slow down.

As soon as they arrived at the club, She ripped off the helmet and threw it at him.

"You asshole, I was terrified!" she said with a big grin.

"I'm sorry, but you have to admit, that it was fun."

"Yeah!" she reluctantly spewed, through a huge smile.

She looked into the side view mirror of the motorcycle.

"Shit, you're right, that helmet messed up my hair."

He pulled out his wallet and gave her five dollars. "Here, there is a bathroom inside if you need to get fixed up. I'll meet you inside. Just let me lock up your helmet."

She smiled and gave him a small kiss on the cheek, then pranced off to the club's entrance.

He melted right there.

"Oh yeah," He stopped her in her tracks, "If the bouncer gives you a hard time, just tell him you're with me. Plus, nobody knows this, but his name is Speck. Call him that and he should let you in."

He watched her graceful gate, swaying her sexy hips back and forth. He took out a cigarette and lit it up. That would give him enough time, so it looked like he came by himself.

She swayed up to the bouncer. She did not think that his name matched his stature. He stood six-feet, five inches tall and weighed at least three hundred pounds.

"Hello," she said trembling.

The bouncer looked down at her and said, "Sorry little girl, this is a twenty-one and over show."

"Oh, I'm with, Billy."

"Really?" The bouncer looked her up and down in total disbelief.

"Yeah, your name is Speck, right?"

The hulk bouncer grinned at her.

"Ha, ha, yeah, only Billy calls me that, and probably the only one that can get away with it too."

She smiled with relief and gave him the five dollars.

"Oh, no cover charge for a pretty young girl like yourself. Go right in. Any friend of Billy's is a friend of mine."

He finished his cigarette and greeted Speck. "Hey, hey there, Bobby. How's it hanging? Looks like you been losing some weight. Have you stopped eating small babies?"

"Hey there, Billy boy. Still the little rascal, I see. Hey, I just let a fine-looking girl in that claims to be with you. But now that I see you, I think she might have pulled a fast one on me," Bobby joked.

"That's a funny one, Bobby. You know what, you are so lucky that you are ten times bigger than me, because otherwise I would wipe the floor with you."

The burley bouncer just smiled, picked him up, and bear-hugged the breath out of him. The giant one squeezed him until he gave in.

"Okay! Okay! I give up, you big fucking bear. You're messing up my hair!"

Bobby put him down and patted him on the back.

In the corner of the bar, a 'reserved' table waited for Billy and The Click. Nobody else sat there except for close acquaintances. The Click sat at the table, anticipating his arrival. He nodded at Hank, letting him know that he acknowledged their presence, he then went over to the bar.

"Hey bartender, can I get some fucking service here or do I have to drink out of the god-damn toilet!"

The bartender twisted around, "Listen fuck-face, if you're talking...Oh, it's you, Billy."

"Wow, do you talk like that to all your customers? Now I know why this place is dead all the time," Billy smiled.

"Yeah, yeah, yeah, what can I get for you?"

"Um, from outside I heard gin and tonic calling me, and I'm not one to say no to a friendly invitation."

The bartender poured his drink. "That will be three-fifty."

"Oh, just put it on my tab, would you, Todd."

"Yeah, yeah, get out of here. You are blocking real, paying customers!"

He grabbed his drink, "I owe you one."

It was an awsome turn-out, a lot of people showed up that night. Billy walked through the crowd and sat in his corner seat.

"Hey Billy, I see you finally made it."

Billy chugged his drink down.

"Well you know Guy, the hair just would not stay today."

"Hey Billy, check it out." Hank grabbed a piece of paper from the table and showed it to him.

"See that girl over there? This is her number. She gave it to me. Huh, huh, who won the bet now?"

Billy looked at the girl then back at Hank.

"Shit Hank, are you serious? That girl looks like she ran through the ugly forest and smashed into every tree she came across. I mean, I shit prettier than that."

Guy laughed at the thought.

Sick boy walked up to the table holding his eye, "What's so funny?"

"Hey, Sick Boy, sit down, grab a beer."

The four boys all sat there, goofing off and drinking. They were having the time of their lives.

"You look kinda cut up there, Sick Boy. What happened?"

"Some cunt bumped into me as I walked in. So I called him out and took care of business. T - C - B, Billy!"

"By the looks of you, it looks like you could have used a little help."

"I know, but these pussies didn't wanna back me up."

"Don't worry, I got your back the next time."

"Me too!"

"Hey, fuck you Hank, I asked you and you said, 'nah.'"

"No, you told me, not asked me, there is a difference."

Sick Boy shook his head, "Whatever."

Guy just sat there with a big-ass smile across his face. He put his head down and snorted another line of coke off the table.

Billy watched Savanna saunter out of the rest room.

"Hey Hank, see that lady over there. Now *that* is a won

bet."

"Isn't that the girl who was with Bradley, that one time at the park?"

"Right you are buddy. Now watch a master at work." Billy grabbed his drink and strolled over to her.

"Watch nothing. The only thing I'm going to watch is you getting shot down!"

"Are you willing to put your money where your mouth is?" Hank asked.

"Yeah, no problem, Sick Boy, if you want me to take all of your money."

As Billy moved in on Savanna, Hank and Sick Boy emptied their wallets and counted out the money they would wager.

Guy started to pour lines of coke out for everyone at the table, he snorted the first one.

"Hey, Savanna, over here!"

"There you are! I thought maybe you left me here."

"No, I would never do anything like that to you. Do you want something to drink?"

"Hum, a gin and tonic sounds nice."

"Hell yeah, that's what I'm drinking too," Billy grabbed her by the hand and lead the way to the bar.

Hank and Sick Boy watched closely, in amazement.

"Hey barkeep, a gin and tonic please."

The bartender turned, "You need another one already Billy?"

"No, this is for my new lady-friend."

Savanna smiled at the bartender.

He poured her drink, "It's on the house."

She grabbed the drink and sipped on it.

The bartender moved close to him, leaned over the bar, and whispered in his ear, "You are a lucky fuck Billy, she's a cutie. Don't fuck it up!"

He smiled with confidence, "Don't worry Todd. You should know that I always come out on top and top is where I want to be tonight," he announced as he admired his beautiful date.

"Let's meet the boys, shall we? Oh yeah, just one last thing. Don't take anything they say seriously. We goof around a lot, that's all."

"It's alright, Billy. I'm sure I'll get along with them."

He held her hand and led the way to the table. It seemed as though he floated a little bit higher that night, all the way up to Cloud Nine.

"Hey bastard's, I'd like you to meet, Savanna."

Hank looked at her in shock.

"Ha! I knew it. Pay up mother-fucker!" Sick Boy pointed at Hank.

She looked at them, a little confused.

Billy quickly gestured at Sick Boy, "Yeah, um, this is Sick Boy with the LOUD MOUTH."

"It is a pleasure, seeing you here, with Billy," Sick Boy gawked at Hank.

"And this is my good friend, Hank."

"Hey." Hank refused to make eye contact with her. He was too pissed-off about losing both bets.

"And the one snorting a White Christmas over there, is Guy."

Guy looked up with coke all over his nose, "Hi. Want a few lines?"

Savanna looked at Billy, uncertainty written all over her lovely face.

"It's alright Savanna, it'll be fun."

She smiled, letting go of her inhibitions.

"Oh hell, what the fuck," she sat down.

Billy grabbed a seat right next to her. He snorted his first line, then his second. Then he sat straight-up.

"Hot dog! That's some good shit!" he started to make a line for her.

Now Hank just stared at her in disgust.

"You know, Savanna, only The Click is suppose to be sitting here."

Savanna smiled at Hank, "I'm...sorry."

"Shut up, Hank! She is with me, alright?"

"No, I'm just saying, if she's in, I'm not cutting my lines shorter. It's coming out of your shit, Billy."

"I know that asshole. It's not like you snort a lot or any at all, for that matter."

A nervous Savanna put her head down and snorted the line.

They all watched her.

Billy grabbed the coke bag out of Guy's hand and threw it at Hank. "Here you go, you whiney bitch."

Hank caught the bag and poured out his cut. He drew himself a huge line trying to impress everyone, then gave the bag to Sick Boy. Sick Boy got so excited, he started to shake. He didn't even bother to pour a line. He just slammed his face into the bag and inhaled.

"Fuck, save some of that for me, dick!"

Guy ripped the bag away from Sick Boy and peeked inside it. "You're a real fucking Jackal, you know that, right?"

"Ha, I'm sorry, I just needed to ease some pain."

Guy shook his head and poured himself the last little bit that was left in the bag.

Billy slammed his empty drink glass on the table and eyed Sick Boy. "Alright Sick Boy, you ready for your drink?"

Sick Boy smiled, "Let's do this!"

Billy pointed at Todd the bartender. "Go over there and order a K - T - F - O."

Sick Boy stood up and leered.

"Ok! I hope I can handle it." Sick Boy joked. He went to the bar and sat on a stool near Todd. "Todd, right?"

The bartender looked at Sick Boy, "What can I do for you?"

"Can I get a 'K - T - F - O?'"

Todd glanced at The Click. They were all smiling, watching the show.

"So you're joining the Click, huh? Open your mouth."

An uncertain Sick Boy felt very uneasy.

Todd grabbed five bottles from under the bar. Gin, rum, whiskey, tequila and vodka.

Sick Boy held his head back with his mouth wide open.

Todd grabbed up all five bottles and poured them into his mouth simultaneously until the mix overflowed onto his lips.

Sick Boy grimaced as his eyes watered up. He shut them and swallowed.

Todd wound up and punched Sick Boy square in the face while his eye's were closed.

He squinted, his eyes rolled back and he fell off the bar stool.

Todd leaned over the bar and looked at Sick Boy, passed out, sprawled on the floor.

"K - T - F - O. Knocked The Fuck Out! Dumb-ass! Now you better leave a tip."

Billy and The Click rollicked with boisterous laughter.

Savanna gasped in horror, and shock, covering her mouth, "Is he gonna be alright?"

"He'll be fine."

The band took the stage and started to play. It was good old, greaser-punk, infectious licks blaring and pulsing through the speakers. Billy looked at Hank, Hank looked at Guy. They all had smiles on their faces, they sprang up and rushed to the dance floor.

"I'll be right back, Savanna. A man's gotta do, what a man's gotta do," he said as he bounced away.

For the next twenty minutes, all the boys were double skanking, pogo-ing and behaving as rowdy as possible. They were always the first to start the mosh pit. Billy took the stage and played guitar and sang harmony on a couple of tunes.

Savanna watched in awe of the boys slam-dancing high-energy, and thought, *What a crazy world I'm in.*

The bouncers carried Sick Boy to the table. He slowly regained consciousness.

Billy, soaked in sweat, tired of dancing and performing for the crowd, he headed back to the table. He sat next to Sick Boy and held his face up to assess the damage. "That's gonna be a nice shiner. Welcome to the club!" he sucked in the heavy stale smoky air, trying to catch his breath.

Sick Boy shook his head and held his hand up to his forehead. "Billy, man....That was *the* best fucking drink I ever had!"

Billy smiled, then turned to Savanna, "Hey, you. What do you think?"

"I love the music, but I think I'll stay back here and listen to it. You are so crazy! I'm impressed, your singing, dancing and guitar-playing is phenomenal. It looked like you were having a blast. You're really talented."

Flattery, baby, will get you..."Yeah, thanks, darlin'. But I need a cigarette break and I wanted to see how you're doing."

"Thank you! I'm doing fine. You can go back out with your friends."

"No, I want to stay with you. Do you need a cigarette or a drink?"

"I can go for a cigarette."

He grabbed the damp cigarette from behind his ear; a quick trick flip with the Zippo and he lit it up, took a drag, then handed the cigarette to Savanna.

She giggled as she eyed the Zippo. "I was wondering what happened to that."

"Yeah, I put it in my pocket last time, by accident. He handed it back to her.

She held it for a few moments and then gave it back to him. "It's yours, in token of my gratitude for taking me away from the bullshit. At least for one night."

"So, have you talked to Bradley lately?"

"Not really, I just told him that I was going out tonight with a friend."

He looked at her, "So, you didn't say anything to him about what we talked about?"

"I just can't do it, Billy. Things are just easier this way."

"Okay...and I'm just *a friend* to you?"

"Of course you are, silly. Wait, you didn't think this was a date, did you?"

He quipped back, "Oh, no, I just...I don't know...I just thought you were going to break up with that guy," he looked away at the band, and his friends on the dance floor enjoying themselves. On the surface you couldn't tell, but he was aching inside. He was always good at hiding his emotions. His plan had backfired in his face. She was still with Bradley and this was not a real date. He chugged his drink, and sat silent, staring into the crowd. The walls closed in and everybody seemed to move in slow motion. The band's music sounded like muffled echoes.

Hank and Guy came back from the dance floor, tired and sweating. "Billy! Where were you out there? ...Hello! Earth to Billy!"

"Oh what? I just...had to take a breather, Hank."

A breather? This pissed Hank off. Billy had never tired before. He had never even seen him take a break before. He thought, *Must be that bitch, Savanna.*

They all sat down and talked about what they had done in the pit. Billy remained quiet, although he feigned laughter and interest in the conversation and the jokes. He was not really paying attention. He could only think of what Savanna said to him and it rolled in his mind over and over again. Suddenly, the bar doors flew open. It was Bradley and his prep slackies. Sick Boy noticed them first as Bradley pointed in their direction.

"Hey Billy, you said you got my back in the next fight, right?"

"Yeah sure, why?"

"Because here it comes," said Sick boy.

He looked up while Bradley pushed his way through the crowd." Billy smiled at Sick Boy and whispered, "We are going to have fun with this one."

"Oh shit!" Savanna tried to hide her face behind her drink.

Bradley and his crew walked up to the table. "I can't believe what I'm seeing. What the fuck are you doing here with these losers, Savanna?"

"I'm sorry Bradley, I just—"

"Not a another word!" Bradley pointed at Sick Boy, "and you, you fucking crazy bastard. That was my buddy that you beat up tonight. I'm going to kill you!"

"A buddy, huh, Bradster? Would you even consider calling him your *butt* buddy?"

The Click laughed.

"Billy, Billy, Billy, now I find you here with my girl. You must have a death wish."

"We are only friends!"

"Shut up, bitch! Just shut the fuck up and get over here," he reached out and grabbed her by the hair.

Billy stood up and pushed him off of her. Hank, Sick Boy, and Guy rose out of there seats. The band stopped playing and the crowd turned to watch the impending fight.

"Maybe she doesn't want to go with you, Bradley."

Bradley's goons got a little bit closer to the table.

"Billy, you have no idea what you're getting into."

Bradley and Billy stood face to face. Bradley faked a punch.

Billy didn't take the bait, he did not flinch.

"Your move, Billy!"

He dug into his pocket for the knife. He pushed Bradley back with one hand and swung with the other gripping the switchblade.

Bradley stumbled back and looked down at his chest. His shirt had been sheared and a trickle of blood leached through. He gazed in disbelief at the wild-eyed ruffian who stood ready, in attack mode, brandishing the knife.

A crazed Sick Boy relished the moment when he saw the emblazoned and bloodied knife.

"That's my uncle's knife! You cut me with my uncle's knife!" Bradley wiped at his bloody chest and stared in shock at the blood on his hand.

"Yeah, that's not the only thing I'm going to do with it," said Billy.

Bradley, in shock, took a few unsteady steps forward and took a swing at him.

Savanna jumped in between them. "Stop it! Just stop! Let's just go home Bradley," she begged, looking at Billy, "I'm sorry, please put the knife away."

"You know you don't have to go."

"Yes I do."

Bradley put his arm over her shoulder and one of his friends for support. The cut was deeper than any of them had thought. The blood poured down his chest.

"Your dead Billy! The cops will be coming for you! And after you get out of jail, I'm going to kill you! This is not over!"

They carried Bradley out the door yelling. Savanna kept gazing back at Billy as he watched her walk out of his life.

The bar's patrons went back to what they were doing. The band began to play after the lead singer yelled out, "Throw out that square cat!"

Billy and the boys sat back down.

"Fuck Billy, you should not have pulled out that knife. The cops are really going to have a field day with this."

"Fuck the cops, Hank! And fuck Bradley! If he calls out the Devil he better be prepared to dance."

"Yeah, that's right! Take no shit from nobody!" Sick Boy stood up and rushed out the front door. He taunted Bradley and his crew as they drove off.

Guy grabbed the almost empty bag of coke and began to lick the residue inside.

Billy walked to the bar, "Hey Todd, can I have a shot of Jameson?"

Todd poured him the shot.

"Thanks Todd, I needed that. Oh yeah! Leave the bottle too."

An unsure Todd commented, "Sure, why not."

"Todd, why don't you tell some good 'ol wise bartender advise."

Todd leaned in across the bar. "You know kiddo, life has it's up's and down's, between that, there is alcohol. Right now alcohol is not the solution, but it is the right answer." Todd walked away to serve other customers waiting for their drinks.

"Short but sweet," Billy shook his head in agreement. He grabbed the bottle and walked back to the table.

"So, what are you going to do now, Billy?"

"I don't know, Hank. I'm just going to finish this bottle

here and see where it takes me."

The band finished their set, and the crowd cleared out. He guzzled the bottle, stood up and wobbled. He struggled to keep his balance. "Alright, I'll see you cats later," he stumbled toward the door.

Hank yelled out, "At least you won the bet!"

"No...no. I didn't," he pushed the door open, and jumped on his motorcycle, jammed down the kick-starter, and tore off down the road.

"Everything just really blew up in my face tonight Jean. Bradley won the girl. She didn't even acknowledge me as a date. And to top if off, I broke my promise to my mom about trying to be good. I can't hide this. She will know when the fucking pigs knock at my door tomorrow."

I don't know what to tell you. You tried, but this element that you live and breathe in, goes against what you are trying to do. Maybe you shouldn't change. Maybe it is not you who is in the wrong, but the world.

"Maybe you're right. It's just...I felt at peace for the first time in my life. I mean I didn't even care that I was with my friends and a good band was playing. I didn't care about what beer I was drinking or the coke I was snorting. It was her, next to me, that made me feel good."

Forget about it. She made up her mind and you are not part of her life. Besides, you still got me. Now let's see how fast we can go.

Billy grinned and twisted back on the throttle. He arrived home in no time at all by taking the straight-away back roads. He reached one hundred thirty miles per hour, but slowed down when he saw flashing blue and red lights in the distance. Three cop cars with their lights on were waiting for him in front of the house.

"Fuck! That fucking Bradley wasted no time, did he? Well, it is time to face the music." He pulled into the driveway as a fire truck and ambulance pulled up behind him.

"What the fuck is going on? All this because of a little scrap."

Billy jumped off his bike and tried to walk into his house.

"Whoa there son! You can't go in there,"said the police officer guarding the front door.

"Fuck you! Take your hands off me, man! This is my home. What's going on? Where's...my mom?" He pushed the officer to the side. He saw a trail of blood that led to his mother's bedroom. "Mom! Mom!" He pushed his way into the house and into her room. Three police officers were on top of his dad, struggling to get him into handcuffs. Billy's mom, a bloody mess, laid off to the side, moaning in pain. He rushed to her side. "Mom! Mom!" He held her in his arms and rocked her back and forth wanting to ease her suffering. Her whole face was swollen, and blood was pouring out of her ears.

"I'm glad...I was able to...see you one last time," she gasped for breath.

"Don't talk like that Mom. You are going to be fine. Can I get some help in here?" he screamed.

The cops wrestled his father to his feet after finally getting the handcuffs on him and then dragged him out to their squad car.

"Billy take care...of yourself...remember I will always be...with you...watching you," her eyes rolled back and closed. She laid motionless in his arms.

"NO! NO! NO!...This can't happen! I need a doctor in here!"

Just then, the EMT's rushed in. They pushed him to the side, "We got it from here," one of them barked.

He stood up and paced back and forth as they worked on his mother. They tried to resuscitate her, but stopped, after several minutes when they could not detect any vital signs.

"What are you doing? She's not back to normal!" he rushed over to her. One of the EMT's held him back.

"She's gone, son. I'm sorry. There is nothing further we can do for her."

He put his head on the guy's shoulder and tears streamed down his face. He became quiet for a couple of seconds, then he pushed off the man in anger and stomped his way outside. His face red with fury, drenched in hate. He kicked the front door open. His father, in handcuffs, leaned against the squad car talking to a cop attempting to garner sympathy.

Billy raced over to him, "MOTHERFUCKER!"

An officer blocked his path.

The mix of cocaine and adrenaline coursed through his veins. It gave him extra strength, as he bull-dozed through the cop, sending him flying back on his ass. He pulled out the knife and tackled his father. They both went flying over the back of the squad car and spilled to the ground. Billy pounced on his chest, and raised his arms above his head.

The drunkard tried to struggle free, but the handcuffs made it impossible.

With fire in his eyes he said, "This is for everything you put Mom through!" Without forethought, he plunged the knife blade to the hilt into his father's forehead. All four-inches of steel disappeared into the terrified man's skull. He stayed there on top of him and watched him twitch.

The police officer stumbled to his feet and ran to them, he tried to pull the enraged son off his father. Another officer ran over to assist. They finally managed to wrestle the boy off.

He spit on his father's lifeless body and kicked at the corpse.

The officers handcuffed him and threw him into the back of the squad car. He just sat there, numbed by an unreal calm, covered in blood.

The news would spread quickly in the small town. All of the neighbors watched from the street. Angel stood there, crying uncontrollably, in total disbelief and shock, hugging Pike. The Click stood next to her; deep despair in their eyes. Billy hung his head as the squad car disappeared into the darkness, to God knows where.

CHAPTER 4

"One fire burns out another's burning, one pain is lessened by another's anguish."
—William Shakespeare, 'Romeo and Juliet,' Act 1, Scene 2

Unbalanced Justice

The squad car arrived at the police station, and the officers ripped Billy out of the back of the car. They dragged him through the front doors of the station and threw him into an interrogation room, and slammed the door shut.

One steel-legged chair, strategically placed in the middle of the room. A single light fixture hung directly above it. A huge mirror covered the wall right in front of him. Billy knew what that was for. He stared into the one-way window, rocking the chair on two legs, back and forth. On the other side of the mirror, Lt. Dan Gip and Officer Jack O'Neil watched Billy, and talked.

"You know this kid, Dan?"

"Yeah, I had a couple run-in's with him before. A real troubled kid. Been to his house for a domestic call once or twice. He's a real smart-ass."

"So what are we going to do? I mean he just saw his mother die and he killed his dad. The judge is going to nail him to the wall, probably for man-slaughter in the first. I kinda feel sorry for this kid."

"Yeah well, if you knew him, you wouldn't. He is what's wrong with society. A plague! Little kids that act like they are in charge of the whole world, bad-asses, who think they can do anything they want. I hope the judge fries him!"

A concerned O'Neil looked at Gip.

"Why do you have such a hard-on for this kid?"

Gip stared at Billy, "No reason. Why? What have you heard?"

"I didn't hear anything. It just seems you hate this kid with a passion."

Gip walked out of the observation room and into the interrogation room.

O'Neil shook his head and followed.

"Well, well, well, if it isn't little Billy Boy. You know, you are going down forever on this one. I don't care about your mother and neither will the judge, I'll make damn sure of that!"

"Oh really? Wait! I remember you. Your name is Sergeant Gimp, right?"

"Laugh all you want boy. I will be laughing last, this time."

"You're not still mad about that little demotion thing are you, Gimp? How is your precious flower of a daughter anyways?" Billy displayed his evil sneer.

Gip's face turned bright red with anger. He jumped across the table, and strangled him to the ground. O'Neil scurried over and pulled him off of the teen.

O'Neil forced Gip back and pushed him out of the door. "He's just a kid God damn it! Calm down and wait outside, I'll handle this."

Billy picked up the chair, brushed himself off and sat back down.

"What was that all about?"

"It's a long story. You must be new on the force. Put it this way, I once knew his daughter all too well. One night he caught us in his bedroom. He got so pissed off, he beat me up pretty bad. He was a Captain at the time, but was demoted because of the *incident*."

"You were the one at Dead Man's Curve that night. I told you to go home."

He grinned at the officer.

"I'm sorry about your mother. I can't imagine what you are going through, but you are going to have to play ball if you want to beat this murder wrap. I've seen the way you behave. The jury is not going to give a rat's ass about some greaser kid who killed his father in cold blood. If you are presentable and play it off as self-defense, you *may* walk."

"What? Why do you care? You don't know me! Anyway, he deserved to die. I'm going to be myself. If the system finds me guilty then we both know what's really wrong with the world."

"What I'm about to say goes against everything that the law stands for. Don't get me wrong, if someone killed my mother, I would hunt that fucker down and kill him myself. But, the letter of the law says—"

Billy stared hatefully at him, "Laws are only good for one thing, to break them."

"So you're just gonna throw your life away? And for what? To look cool?"

"I don't care. I have nothing to go back to. Maybe I'm better off here, caged like a fucking animal!"

O'Neil shook his head in disbelief, "Well maybe when you stop feeling sorry for yourself and stop blaming the world around you, you will be reasonable and want to talk," O'Neil walked out of the bleak, cramp room.

Gip then stormed back in, grabbed Billy, and dragged him to a holding cell and threw him in, "Sweet dreams you little cock-sucker!"

"Say hello to your daughter for me, will ya!" Billy went to the empty cot and lied down. He stared at the ceiling wondering what to do and what would become of him. A tear rolled down his face, he thought about his mother. He eventually fell into an uneasy sleep.

Maybe tomorrow I will wake up from this nightmare and all of this reality shall become a dream.

***

Two weeks passed begrudgingly. A clang on the cell bars woke him.

"It's time for your court appearance, Billy."

He sat up and looked at O'Neil, then at the man standing next to him.

"Who's this?"

"Hi, my name is David Steel. I'm your attorney," he removed a folder from his brief case. "Let's see now, Billy is it? Oh, oh! Murder? I never had a murder case before."

Billy peered at the exuberant fresh face. *Oh shit, I'm fucked!* "Is there any possibility that I can represent myself?"

"Don't worry, I know, I'm young and this is my first felony case, but I'm going to work really hard to get you free."

"You know Billy, a man who represents himself in court has a *fool* for a lawyer," O'Neil cautioned, as he motioned Billy to come out of the cell.

His head hung low as he walked out of the cell. "Alright let's get this over with."

Gip burst through the gate and wrapped full body chain restraints on him.

"Is that all really necessary?" Steel inquired.

Perhaps Gip wanted him to look dangerous in front of the judge.

In the courtroom, sat Angel, and Pike. They were accompanied by Hank, Guy, and Sick Boy. Savanna too, hid in a far corner. He smiled at them, but it was not real. It seemed fake. He knew that the book was going to be thrown at him in this small town mentality courtroom.

The bailiff walked into the courtroom, "All rise for the Honorable Judge of the Juvenile Court, Richard Taker."

The judge walked up to the bench, sat down and told everyone to 'be seated.'

The prosecutor stood up and approached the judge, "Your Honor, this boy has a history of violence, drinking under age, and use of narcotics. Much older men that I have prosecuted have had lesser criminal records, and fewer run-ins with law enforcement than this, *minor*. First, your Honor, the State moves that this defendant be tried as an adult, and then, and *only* then will the State entertain a motion for an indictment of second degree manslaughter." The prosecutor sat back down and glared at Billy.

David Steel stood up and asked permission to approach the bench.

Judge Taker gestured his approval.

"Your Honor, Billy may not be a model young teenager..."

The kid cracked an evil smile.

"But he has had a rough childhood. His late father beat him many times while in a drunken stupor. Not to mention, beating and killing his mother in cold blood.

"The police may have been to his house a few times, but no legal action was ever taken. This child's first reaction was to protect his mother's well-being, and, in self-defense, your Honor. He may have acted spontaneously, emotionally. But, he is for all intent, purposes, and in the eyes of the law, a child. I move that the court orders young Billy into a juvenile facility for counseling and rehabilitation for this unfortunate occurrence. Thank you, your Honor." Steel sat back down at the table for the defense. He patted Billy on the back with a somber look on his face as he searched the judge's eyes for leniency.

"Damn, you sounded pretty good out there," Billy commented.

"Sshh!" Steel cautioned.

"Your Honor! Good grief. Really..." the prosecutor sounded incensed.

Taker pondered Steel's motion as he skimmed through Billy's rap sheet.

"I see this case is going to be awkward and complex. It does not matter how I rule, no one wins, not this troubled young man, and not our community. I'll entertain arguments at this time from both learned counsels."

For the next two hours the lawyers engaged in a philosophic battle of wits and law, while the judge absorbed it all. It didn't look good for Billy. Lt. Gip provided so many police doc-

uments against him, it seemed as though he had kept a personal diary focused on him, and had saved it for the right occasion. All the evidence against him had been laid out for the judge.
David Steel leaned over and said, "I'm not going to lie to you. I don't think this is going to go our way."

"I could've told you that the day I was born," Billy snorted.

The judge nodded at the youth before rendering his decision. "I just want to say I'm sorry about the death of your mother, young man. That, not withstanding, I must follow the rule of law at all times, regardless of my personal feelings, or opinion. I cannot *legally* condone what you did. However, in the eyes of the State, you *are* a child, and you will be adjudicated as one. You are a troubled and lost kid that requires strict guidance, professional counseling, and other rehabilitative efforts. Therefore, William Robert Bomm, I sentence you to three years in the Rockyards Boys Home. I hope, and pray, that you get the help you need and that you can eventually find peace within yourself and live a productive life. It is so ordered. Case dismissed," Taker slammed his gavel down in finality.

"Your Honor! Please! My God! How can *this* be justice?" the prosecutor railed against the court's decision.

"I have ruled, counselor, and I said, *case dismissed*."

During the judge's speech Billy sat in silence, never said a word or even blinked an eye. He hated the legal system, blamed it for all of the problems in the world.

"We *could* appeal, Billy, but I have to be honest with you; an appeal could very well backfire on us. It could be decided that you should be tried as an adult for first degree murder, then you may have the death penalty looming over your head. Really, son, you should be pleased. All things considered, the court's decision is a lenient one. The time will pass quickly, you'll see."

Yeah, right, it ain't your ass going to prison, motherfucker! Shit! Nevertheless, he knew Steel was probably right.

O'Neil escorted him back to the dungeon-esque cell.

He kept his head down so he did not have to look at The Click and the girls. He passed Gip only to look up and give him that grin.

"You got off lucky, punk. I'll see you inside."

"I'm looking forward to it Gimp!"

***

That next morning he was transported to the R.B.H., a three hour drive from his hometown. Rockyards, a boy's home, more prison-like than a school. It had a reputation for it's brutal, territorial gangs, and the guards were corrupt and ruthless. The facility was rundown, and as he walked passed the on-looking inmates, it appeared to him that their spirits had been broken. Nothing but lost looks in their eyes. Billy kept his head down as he continued to shuffle along. Their faces were a reminder of the hell which awaited for him. Lt. Gip escorted him personally, he noticed the look on Billy's face. He managed to maintain his composure and facade of cool.

Gip removed the leg irons, "This is your hotel room punk!" He pushed him hard into the cell and slammed the door shut.

He regained his balance and ran back to the bars, he clamped down on them hard. They stood face to face; only the steel bars stood between them.

Gip whispered, "I'm glad your fucking mother died, she could never suck cock right, anyway," he punched Billy through the bars, sending him flying back.

Billy wiped the blood from his nose and yelled, "This ain't over gimp! Not by a long shot!"

"I see the lieutenant doesn't like you much," a voice said from the top bunk. A young man, smoking a cigarette, covered in tattoos, and wearing a 'wife-beater' said.

"Yeah, I fucked his goody-two-shoes daughter pretty raw in his own bed, and ever since then, he's had kind of a hard-on for me," Billy admitted.

"Are you serious? That is the reason I'm in here," he took a drag off his cigarette.

"I'm sorry, I didn't catch your name."

"Didn't throw it out...It's Dean."

"Got a extra cigarette Dean?"

He picked up his pack and tossed it to him.

"Thanks! Cool, *Lucky's* and everything. My name's Billy."

"I know who you are. Everybody here knows of Billy. Greasers like us have to stick together man. You're going to be popular here if all the stories are true about you."

"Yeah, well, don't believe everything you hear, Dean. What are you in for?"

Dean laughed, "We have a lot in common. Supposedly, I'm here for raping the Gip's precious little daughter, but I didn't rape that whore. Make a long story short, I popped her cherry and her dad finds out. Then, like a little bitch she tells her dad that I raped her so she doesn't get in any trouble and comes out looking like a good girl."

"Wow! That is pretty fucked-up man. I feel for you. Damn, I had no idea that Gip's daughter was such a whore," Billy puffed on his cigarette. "How much time you got left?"

"I got sent here when I was fifteen, just like yourself. I've served only three years of my six year sentence, so far. It looks like we will be getting out of this fucking place at about the same time." Dean nodded and lit up another cigarette.

"So...I got a rep in here, already? Tell me about my advantage."

"Well, nobody's gonna fuck with you here because of two reasons: you're in here for murder and you will get a lot of respect for that, plus, you got me and my crew backin' you up."

"Why are you backing me up?"

"Word travels around here even though we are locked up. I heard you can really press Bradley's buttons."

"Bradley? You mean that poser, cocksucker. You know that guy too?"

"Yeah, that cocksucker. I know him, not by choice. My cousin is going out with him. She won't admit to it, but I think he beats on her."

"Wait...Wait...Is her name, Savanna?"

"Yeah, you know her?" Dean asked.

Billy smiled, "Yeah, I know her, she's the reason I cut up Bradley, I mean, one of the reasons."

"What do you mean, are you seeing her?"

"No, obviously not. But I can tell you one thing, he does hurt her in more ways than you could imagine."

"I knew it! I cannot wait to get out! I am going to fuck that guy up!"

"Yeah, I got a couple of scores to finish too." An image of the lieutenant passed through Billy's mind.

Dean smiled, "You know what Billy, another thing that is gonna piss me off, when I do get out, I'll be twenty-one years old."

"Yeah, that sucks."

"No, I mean it is going to be hard to screw little girls."

"What? Eighteen is a good age for legal girls."

"Hell no! You gotta get them young, I'm talking about eleven-teen and twelve-teen." Dean's fingers ran back through his greasy black hair.

Billy cringed slightly, "You don't think that's kinda young?"

"Fuck no. It's like my grandfather used to say, 'if there is grass on the field and a pitcher's mound. Play ball!'"

"There is something wrong with you. You know that, right?"

"Man, as soon as they get their license, they are too old and independent."

Billy shook his head as he cracked up. The boy's continued to talk all through that night, telling stories about their messed up lives.

The next morning they were woken by the loud-speaker "Breakfast time! Move it or lose it!"

The cell doors opened and everyone stood in single file, outside of their cells. Billy walked out yawning and stood off to the side, out of line.

One of the correction officers approached the disobedient inmate. "And what the fuck do you think you are doing? Get in line, right now!"

Billy looked at him but ignored the order.

"I'm talking to you, boy!" the guard pushed him.

"Look if you yell in my fucking ear one more time I'm gonna..."

The guard looked him up and down, "What the fuck do you think you're going to do, squirrel?"

He just stared back at him then got in line. The guard watched and smiled. He had a disturbing grin.

Dean quickly snuck in line, close to Billy. "You should not piss off that guard. His name is Dozer, but everyone calls him 'Mr. Bull.' Watch yourself, he's one of those *funny fellows*. He fights for the pink team."

Billy looked befuddled.

"Dude! He is a fudge packer! You know, he likes to play butt darts. You don't want to get thrown in the hole by him. I've heard of stories that he visits kids in the hole and it is not pretty, if you know what I mean."

"That is fucking sick!" Billy spat on the ground next to Dozer as the guard continued to stare.

'Gruel' as the inmates called it, was being served. Billy and Dean grabbed their food and sat at a table.

"Okay, this place breaks down into specific groups. It is crucial that you know these things. I mean, you don't want to bump heads with the wrong person. I got pull, but we can't fight whole gangs. You see those guys at the table to the far left? Those are the Brothers, Inc. Most of them are just straight-up niggers, but I'm cool with the other brothers. To the far right is the complete opposite; the white-power, skin-head Nazi motherfuckers. I know the leader, the gang likes to be called Adolph's Youth, for reasons we both know. They are also the ones with the drugs, so that is who you deal with if you want any. Right in front of us sits the Cholos. Cool bunch of Mexicans, but not the shiniest apples on the tree. Sitting behind us are the Sing Dragons, most of the members are Vietnamese. They are growing fast in population and it's hard to keep any relationship with them. The Sing Dragons are the biggest gang in here and they keep to themselves. Then there is us; a bunch of misfit rejects. Greasers and punks that society doesn't want to roam the streets. We have no gangs, we're just bad-ass dudes, and others like to follow us. All the rest of the kids in here are called 'worms.' They stay out of everyone's way. They're here just to serve their time and then go back to their normal lives. They do not exist, therefore; they are 'worms,' nobody notices them."

Billy's mind wandered as he tried to take it all in.

"Now, let's meet the twins, the Smack Brothers," Dean whistled the brothers over.

They came and sat on either side of Billy. The brothers were twins but different in size. Jimmy was short in stature compared to his larger brother.

"This is Jimmy Smack, he's in for arson."

"Hey Billy, glad to meet you, I'm looking forward to burning anything you ask me to." He had a nasty scar across his face and an unnerving twitch in his right eye and right hand.

Billy mused, *That kid's elevator does not go to the top floor.*

"And over here is, Max Smack."

"I h-h-h-hear-r-r-d a-a-a-a lot a-a-a-ab-b-b-out you B-B-B-illy."

He chuckled inside himself, not about Max's stuttering, but about Max's hair. It looked like he cut it himself. Max didn't have the best pompadour of the group.

"Yeah, Max has a little stutter problem, but you'll get used to it," Jimmy turned to his brother and said, "Isn't that right you stuttering bastard!"

"F-f-f-f-f-f-fuck you, y-y-y-you a-a-a-asshole!"

"Yeah, yeah, I love you too baby," Jimmy mimed a kiss.

"That's a nasty scar you got, who cut you?"

Jimmy caressed his scar and answered, "I don't know actually. We were in a rumble awhile back. There were fists and feet flying everywhere. The next thing I know, I was lying on the ground bleeding. The last thing I remember is one of Bradley's guys hovering over me."

"Y-y-y-yeah, th-h-hat f-f-fucking B-B-Bradley is g-g-g-going t-t-t-to get it-t-t-t w-w-when," Max cranked his head to the side as he struggled to get out the last few words, "we get out!"

"Max, for the love of god, don't talk, you're embarrassing me."

"I'm g-g-g-going to b-b-beat you w-w-w-where you s-s-stand if you k-k-k-keep m-m-m-m-messing with me."

"Alright then Popeye. Anyways..."

A frustrated Max became angry.

"Okay that's enough, leave your brother alone. You see, we all have something in common here. It isn't by accident that you became my cellmate. I pulled a few strings. We have strong connections, also. That is why I'm making this proposition to you."

"I'm listening."

"Let's join together. Your infamous Click and me and my boys. Together we can bring Bradley down and take over that town. What do you say?"

Billy looked at Dean and the Smack boys, he then looked all around the stark room and into the bleak faces, he said, "Let's do it!"

They all smiled and laughed. They told each other stories about their encounters with Bradley and his preps. Billy told them that he called him, *Bradster,* and that really pissed him off.

***

Three months passed since he began serving his sentence. He had seen the worst this place had to offer, he began to slip into a world of loneliness and despair. He did have Dean and his boys to keep a barren smile on his face, now and then, but it was not enough. His whole world and everything he loved had been taken or stolen away from him. Every night, two tears rolled down his face. One for his mother and the other for Savanna. Dean watched him sink into a mild state of depression, he tried to help him see the positive side of things, but it was no use. Dean could not stand to see this dreary side of him, so he made one last attempt. He wrote a letter and hoped the receiver would respond.

One week later, Mr. Bull made a visit to Billy and Dean's cell. "Wake up pretty boy, you got mail."

Billy sat up in his bed.

Mr. Bull threw him a letter and smacked his lips together.

He grabbed the letter, and ignored Mr. Bull while he opened it, he thought, *I wonder who actually cares about me, enough to write. It's probably Angel.* To his surprise, the letter was from Savanna. The look on his face was one of utter elation.

"Dean! Dean! Savanna wrote me!"

"Oh did she?" Dean teased.

"Thanks, I know you had something to do with this."

"No problem." Dean leaned his head back on the pillow.

Dear Billy,

I hope you get this letter. My cousin wrote me about a week ago and told me that you guys are cellmates. He's a good guy, but sometimes he can be a sexist pervert. I just want to say that I'm sorry about that night. I didn't mean to hurt you and I do care about you. Even though it was a short time we spent together, I had a blast, and hopefully when you get out we can do it again. Write me back so I know how you are doing. I have to go now and get ready, Bradley is taking me out tonight and I have to look pretty for him. Hope to hear from you soon.

Love,
Savanna

His face lit up with excitement. He read the letter over and over again, consciously editing out the references to Bradley.

"Well, what did she say?"

He put down the letter, "She does care about me and she did have a good time with me. Oh, she also said that you are a pervert."

"What?"

Billy smiled and laid back on his bed. He read the letter one more time.

"Damn, you really like my cousin, don't you?"

"This letter is everything I wanted to hear from her, except for that Bradley part toward the end. Quick! Give me a pencil and paper, I want to to write back to her."

Dean tossed him a pencil and some paper. Ever since that day, he buried himself in writing to her. It was his way of escaping the horrid place. They had really gotten to know each other over the months, by writing back and fourth.

Day 167,

Dear Journal,

I'm starting this journal because writing is a good way to keep me out of trouble in here. Believe me, trouble is not a hard thing to find. I have found a new happiness in writing to Savanna. She has told me so much about herself and I can't wait to get out. She has told me that life would be different if I was there. Bradley is getting worse, and she can't handle it anymore. I wrote her a poem straight from my heart, and I would send it to her, but the timing must be right when I give it to her. I am not ready for her to know how I feel about her, yet.

"Hey, what are you writing?"

"Oh, oh...nothing, Dean," he put his journal away quickly.

"Look alive, Billy boy! You've got a visitor."

Mr. Bull appeared out of nowhere.

He stood up and walked out of the cell. On the way out, Mr. Bull slapped his ass. He pivoted around, "If you fucking touch me again there's gonna be two hits. I hit you and you hit the floor!"

Mr. Bull smiled at him with a predatory look.

He walked into the visitor's room and sat down. The door swung open; it was Hank.

"Well, there you are fucker!"

Billy went over to his friend and gave him a hug.

Mr. Bull watched them and smiled lustfully.

"What's his deal?"

"Trust me, you do not want to know. So, how the fuck

have you been?"

"How have I been? Fuck Billy, you're the one in this place. I can't really complain."

"Yeah, you're right. So how is everybody?"

"Well, not too good. Bradley has been getting away with a lot of shit. Me and Sick Boy don't have enough influence over everybody to stop him."

"Where's Guy?"

"You didn't hear? He should be joining you soon. After you left he started to use way too many drugs and his dad kicked him out of the house again; that really sent him over the edge. He got carried away! One night he was picked up by some cops while running down the street naked and yelling like a mad man. He had a rag on him that smelt like paint thinner. Anyway, you should see him inside here soon."

Billy shook his head.

"How about, Angel?"

"I don't fucking know. I saw her once and she looked really depressed. Oh, she did want me to tell you something. She said that the reason she does not visit or write to you is because she does not want to see you like this. It's easier to think that you are on a vacation or something. That chick is weird."

He leaned in on Hank, and whispered, "Yeah, well don't worry. I met some cool cats in this place. When I get out we will take the town back. I promise you that."

"That's enough time for you sweet cakes," Mr. Bull ripped him out of his seat and pushed him back to the cellblock.

Hank yelled, "Why don't you pick on someone your own size, you fucking faggot!"

Mr. Bull shoved him back into his cell, "I'll tell your boyfriend that you said, bye!"

"I swear, if that fucker man-handles me one more time, I'm going to snap."

"Don't let it get to you."

He stared out of the cell drenched in hate.

"So, who visited you?"

"It was my good friend, Hank. You know, I talked to you

about him. He said that one of my boys should be coming here soon. So keep an eye out for him. His name is, Guy."

"Not a problem."

"Hey Dean, do you think you can use your connection to get Guy in the same cell with the Smack Brothers?"

"Yeah, no problem. Why?"

"I know Guy, if he is not with some friends. He tends to get depressed. I think that the Smack Brothers will keep him entertained."

That next morning, a new group of inmates came through the prison doors. Billy spotted Guy and nodded at him. Guy looked horrible. He was skinny and pale.

"Dean! There he is, over there. Did you make the arrangements?"

"Come on, what's my name? I also told the Smack Brothers to take care of him and update him on the way things work around here."

"Good, thanks. I don't know how he'll react to this place and without being able to use drugs."

"He's got a little drug problem, huh?"

"Shit Dean, that's like saying, the Pope has a little Catholic problem. The boy snorted Ajax one time because he did not have coke. He was picking blood boogers for a week."

the laughed as they watched Guy trudge down the hall-way. Although, Billy was truly concerned about his friend.

Chapter 5

"The worst comes to the worst."
—Thomas Middleton, 'The Phoenix,' Act IIISC. 1.IBID

Anarchy

Day 431,

I think it is easy to lose time, and your sanity in here. I have no idea how long I have been in for and how long till I get out. Savanna has become my salvation in this place. I have found a peace by writing and talking with her. I have told her about this place and it's violence. She tells me it's all just macho bullshit and that I should stay clear from it. There is too much violence in this world already. She has visited me a few times and she is getting more beautiful every time I see her. She came to visit one time and had a black eye. She claimed she fell down, but I know better. I want to tell her how much I love her and what she is doing to me, but I'll save that for a better time. Maybe when I am a better person; a person that she would consider being with. Guy is fitting in here, though he does complain sometimes about the Smack Brothers. He tells me they are sick in the head. He also said that Mr. Bull is giving him a hard time lately. I told him the same thing Dean told me; just ignore it. It's good advice. I don't know how, but I know that I am going to get the last laugh. Dean and I have been getting to know the gangs. As we feared, this place is too crowded and a race war has started. Right now, there are small, isolated fights. In time, this place will blow up and when it does, my reputation will be out the door and it will be every man for himself.

The following morning found Billy, Dean, and the Smack Brothers sitting out on the prison field, watching a game of football. It was the Brothers Inc. versus The Cholos.

Some of the spectators in the bleachers were Adolph's Youth. The game went smoothly, there had not been any fights, yet. The score was fourteen to seven, Brothers Inc., leading. The rules were simple: there were none, you played until you could not play anymore. After the last score, the Brothers Inc. punted the ball and one of the Cholos, named Roberto, caught it. He started to run down the field. It looked good, he broke tackles and dodged flying bodies, but then he ran into a brick wall named Crusher, a gigantic man-boy. He stood six feet four inches tall and weighed well over three hundred and fifty pounds. Roberto crashed hard. He could not walk off the field by himself. The Inc. all high five'd each other and reveled in the moment.

Adolph's Youth yelled, "Yeah, kill that spic! Wet-back!"

The Cholos' anger boiled and the tension built. Billy sensed the potential explosive atmosphere. He stood up and walked onto the field.

"No, fuck you! That fat bastard jumped on my homie after he was down, *esé*." The leader of the Cholos jammed his finger into one of the brother's faces.

"Well, I'm sorry if your little beaner could not get passed our Crusher."

Crusher smiled and laughed.

"What? What did you just call one of my homies?" The Cholos' leader challenged, as he closed in on the brother's face.

"I said, if your fucking orange, selling ass didn't—"

"Whoa! Whoa! Who do you think you are talking to? You fucking tar-baby!"

The two gang leaders stood face-to-face yelling at each other.

Billy squeezed himself between them and pushed them apart, "Look it was a fair tackle and now you are one man short, which I can cover. No harm, no foul. Okay?"

Out of respect, the Inc. backed off and the Cholos accepted him onto their team. They broke up and went back to their respective field positions. Billy and the Cholos huddled up and called their next play.

Guy walked down the side of the field and sat next to Dean and The Smack Brothers. "Hey Dean, is that Billy out there?"

"Yeah Guy, looks like Billy is doing his good deed for today. I've got a question for you Guy, you knew Billy most of your life, right? I just can't figure him out. Sometimes he is a hardcore son of a bitch and other times, he does things like this. I don't get it."

"Let me tell you something, I've known Billy since childhood and he's always been a rough neck, and everybody just loves to hate him. As far as I can see, he's a great friend who's always got your back. His only problem is..."

"Girls! Right?" Dean blurted.

"Bingo! I would never tell him this to his face, but he is pussy-whipped. I saw him around his mother, I thought maybe he was a mama's-boy, but when he is around girls, in general, he changes his tone. The only thing I would say is we've got to watch out for him. I hope it won't happen, but I fear one day we'll lose him to some chick."

"Girls are only good for one thing, Guy. They are all a bunch of whore's, they just don't know it yet."

"He's gonna learn the hard way that girls come and go, but your friends are forever."

"Bro-s before ho-s!"

Jimmy interrupted the boys conversation.

Dean turned to watch the game.

The Smack Brothers just laughed.

"Billy once told me that you don't speak much, Guy. You seem pretty talkative today."

"Ha, I guess the drugs are outta my system, Jimmy. I feel like actually playing some football. I'm all hyper!"

"Oh shit, I can't let this happen. Quick! Get this dude some drugs!"

Jimmy smiled.

Guy stood up and galloped onto the field.

"Hey Billy, let me in on some of this action."

He hesitated, "Okay, ah, are you feeling alright, Guy?" he twisted Guy's head to the side and examined his eyes.

Guy pushed him away, "Yeah, never better!"

Soaked in sweat, Billy left the field and sat down, "Whew! That was a good fucking workout," he said in a winded voice."

Dean was still trying to figure him out, he looked into his eyes, wanting to piece the puzzle together, "So, you still writing to Savanna?"

He paused for a second, and mumbled, "Yeah, occasionally, why?"

"Oh, no reason."

Billy focused on the game, concerned about his friend on the field.

Dean continued to stare at him, trying to understand.

Meanwhile out on the field, The Cholos had the ball. They snapped it and handed it off to Guy, he cut to the left and then he had a break-away in front of him. He ran as if his life depended on it. He raced toward the end-zone. Lorenzo, the fastest Brothers Inc., gained ground on him. Thirty yards... twenty yards...ten yards. Lorenzo then popped him from behind.

He clipped him. Guy's knees folded and his chin slammed into the grass.

Both teams anticipated trouble and ran to the sprawled out Guy. The Brothers Inc. and the Cholos were again in each other's faces and the yelling escalated.

Adolf's Youth screamed, "Kill the niggers!"

Billy and the boys stood up and ran to Guy's aid.

The guards watched intensely.

"What is your fucking problem!" Guy yelled at Lorenzo.

"Fuck you, honky! If you can't take the heat, get your white-ass out of the kitchen!"

"Really?" Guy replied, zipping a punch to Lorenzo's face, splitting his lip open.

A startled Lorenzo spat the blood out and then tackled Guy. They rolled around on the ground grasping, pinning, and punching each other.

Two gun shots echoed over the crowd and they all scattered.

Mr. Bull held his rifle high in the air. He peered at Guy and Lorenzo on the ground, out of breath. He pried them apart and stood them up. He took one look at Lorenzo and then turned to Guy. A wicked smile crossed his face, "Alright Guy, now your ass is mine!" He let Lorenzo go.

"Wait! He didn't start it. It was that black bastard Lorenzo!" said someone from the on-lookers. Dean, Billy and the Smack Brothers stood still, enraged by hate for the guard. It did not matter what really happened, Mr. Bull was a sick, degenerate and now he had his chance to throw one of Billy's boys in the hole. As Mr. Bull dragged Guy away, he passed by Billy and whispered in his ear, "I would gladly trade him for you, sweetie."

"If you touch him, fat man...Hell! I do not even have to finish this sentence."

Mr. Bull smiled at him, yanking Guy along, kicking and screaming.

"Don't worry, man, those stories are rumors. Probably made-up, so people will fear Mr. Bull."

"Yeah, I hope you're right, Dean. I hope you are right."

Billy and the boys walked off the field, and back to the day room.

Day ???

Dear journal, chaos and mayhem have a new home here. Nobody in this place gets along. Guy has been in the hole for a long time. I'm worried about him. I know he is going crazy in there, but I can't help him. Savanna wrote me last week, she says she wants to just leave town, and not look back. Bradley and her parents are pressuring her, and I want to take her far away from this bullshit and her bullshit, and have a normal life with her...

Dean interrupted his lettter-writing, Would you stop writing, I've got something I want to tell you. I think you should sneak in to see Guy in the hole. You should not forget about him. It's a lonely place in there."

"Oh shit, you're right. I keep forgetting to go. I'll go right after I'm done with this."

Dean shook his head and laid back on his bed.

Despite his promise, he never visited Guy in the hole. All his free time went into writing to Savanna. Three months passed before Guy obtained his release out of the hole. He would never be the same again.

The lunch bell rang and the cell doors slid open. Billy, Dean and the Smack Brothers filed into the cafeteria and sat at their table.

"So how is he?"

"Um, he seems alright. He didn't say anything when he came into the cell this morning."

"N-n-n-no B-B-Billy, he l-l-looked, l-l-l-looked out of it."

"Shut up Jimmy! No he didn't, he just looked kinda ...lost, perfectly normal, just getting out of the hole and everything."

"Look, here he comes now," Dean nodded.

A quiet Guy sat down next to Billy.

"So, um, Guy, how are you?"

He did not respond, he just nibbled at his food.

"Okay? Um, Guy are you are alright?" he nudged his pale, and much thinner friend, but still no response.

Dean then tried to get a reaction, "Come on, it wasn't that bad."

Guy stood up, "No, it was worse!" he then walked over to the Adolph Youth's table and sat next to the leader.

Billy watched in amazement.

"Hey Jason, I need a fix," Guy looked around suspiciously.

"How's it going there, young white American? I saw what happened to you before you went into the hole. Fucking niggers! They think they own the place. I hope my services were helpful to you when you were in."

"Whatever Jason, do you got the stuff or what?"

"Calm down Guy, I got the shit. Remember we are your white brothers in here."

Jason slipped Guy enough coke to last a day or two.

"How much do I owe you?"

"Nothing, for right now. I'll get back to you."

Guy looked at him bewildered but grateful, he walked away with the hidden coke in hand.

Another week passed and Guy contined to deteriorate. He used more and more drugs. Billy's attempts to talk to him failed over and over again. Guy started to hang around with the Youth. One day at lunch, Jimmy told Billy how Guy's drug usage had escalated out of control. Billy glanced at the Youth's table and saw Guy with his head down. He decided to trespass on their territory to check on his friend.

Dean grabbed him.

"You're not going to do what I think you are gonna do, are you?"

"I'm just going over there to talk," he said coolly, and then strolled over to the Youth's table.

"How is it going, Billy? Have you come here to fight along with your fellow white brothers or is this only a social call."

"I'm here just to talk to Guy, Jason."

Guy looked up at him.

"Maybe Guy doesn't want to talk with you," an eerily composed Jason opined.

"Maybe you should let Guy speak for himself!"

Every Youth member at the table stood up, except for Jason.

"You have no idea what you are getting into. I got ways to hurt you so bad, that it will make your mom's death look like a stroll through the park."

Billy grabbed Jason's shirt and pulled him out of his chair, "Yeah, keep on thinkin' that!"

They attempted to stare each other down.

"Hey! If you boys are going to play, play nice!" Mr. Bull ordered.

Jason nodded his gang off.

Billy redirected his attention on Guy and sat down next to him. "What is wrong with you? Why are you hanging with these fucks? Come on man, talk to me!"

A teary-eyed Guy asked, "What the fuck you want from me? Huh? What do you want me to say? What the fuck do you want me to do?"

"Just talk to me, Guy. Like old times."

Guy swiped at his eyes, "It will never be like old times again. I...I tried to stop him, but he was too strong!"

Billy sat quiet, he really had nothing to say, and as hard as he tried, he couldn't imagine what Guy had gone through in solitary.

"What was so important that you couldn't help me see it through?"

He could not tell him the reason; because of his preoccupation with Savanna, he did not make the time.

Guy stared at his friend for a moment and then stood up and walked off.

Billy realized that this place ripped up everybody, from Guy, to even, Savanna. He sat there, hate in his eyes, in his heart. He stroked his chin a few times and then grinned. He quietly stood up and walked back to his cell. A few minutes later, Dean followed. The cell bars vibrated and the door slammed shut. Billy was lied in his bunk and stared at the ceiling. A strange calm enveloped him.

"Um, what happened? What's going on?"

"Don't worry, I will take care of everything. We all need to get out of this place."

"What? Are you talking about, a break out?"

"Oh yeah, and a whole lot more." Billy smiled and grabbed a piece of paper. He started to write. He stayed up the whole night writing. Nothing interrupted his concentration. He woke Dean out of a dead sleep to ask him a few questions.

"Hey, Dean! Wake up. I need some dirt on the Sing

Dragons."

"Huh? What? Damn it, Billy! I was just dreaming of Susie Gibbins."

"Dude, the preachers thirteen year old daughter? What is wrong with you?"

"Yeah, you're right, she is kinda old."

Dismayed, Billy stared at Dean with a half-smile, "You've got a problem. Now...what do you have on the Dragons?"

"Well, let me see. Like I said, they stick to themselves so it is hard to get inside their circle. The only thing I know, one of them's in for double homicide. He's not in regular circulation like us. He spends all his time in the hole."

"Perfect! That is the last piece of the puzzle, thanks."

"What the fuck you working on?"

"You will see in a short time. Let's just say it's going to be fun."

Dean threw the covers over his head, "Well I'm going back to sleep. Maybe if I'm lucky I will dream now about Susie's younger sister," he thrilled himself to sleep.

Billy turned off the lamp and drifted off to sleep as well. *Good night, Savanna. I'll be seeing you soon.*

***

The next day Billy used the pay phone and called Sick Boy.

"Talk to me."

"Hey cunt, how are you?"

"Is that you, Billy?"

"In the flesh."

"Fuck, I haven't heard from you in a long while. I thought you might've forgotten about us."

"Well, I've told you about that 'thinking' thing. It's not for you," he joked.

"Yep, same old Billy. So what's up?"

"Well, I called to tell you that I'm getting out tomorrow."

"Um, okay, I thought—"

"Tah. Tah. Tah. You said that word again."

"Fuck you, I mean I was at the hearing. You got sentenced for three years. It has only been one and a half."

"Wow has it been that long?" his mind wandered off, *Where has the time gone anyway?*

"Hey Billy, you still there?"

"Yeah, yeah, I'm here. No, I'm getting out tomorrow one way or the other. I would call Hank, but I know he would not be up to what I am going to ask you to do."

"I know what you're getting at. So what you need?"

"A truck and a chain. Can you handle?"

"Consider it done."

"Well, I'll see you tomorrow afternoon, in front of the barbed-wire fence at 1:38 sharp. Not a second before or after!" Billy hung up the phone and walked out onto the field. "Well, it's time to abuse my power." He began to put his plan into affect. He walked over to the Youth's hang out, to converse with Jason.

"You have a lot of balls coming over here. You know I could have you seriously beaten right now and you wouldn't have anywhere to run."

"Now, that would not be very nice Jason, since I came over here to say I'm sorry, and I've got some useful information for you."

"Am I hearing you correctly? Billy says he is *sorry*?"

"Yeah, you know, but don't expect this to happen ever again."

"So what is so important?"

He put his arm around Jason and walked off talking to him in a soft voice. "I'm telling you this because I hate those coon bastards."

Jason started to laugh, "I knew it! You do have a little Hitler in you."

"I heard from a bunch of the Brothers Inc. that they are going to take the drug-pushing away from the Youth. I don't want to buy my drugs from fucking monkeys! You hear what I am saying?"

Jason stopped and thought for a second. "Those fucking

niggers. I knew it! You can never trust those niggers! Thanks. Don't worry, those god-damn jungle-bunnies aren't taking over nothing."

"I hope you're right Jay, because I also heard that the take-over will happen out here on the field, tomorrow, 1:30 sharp. So be prepared."

"Oh, we will be ready. I'm telling all the Youths and the Youth's followers about this. If they want a fight, they are going to get one."

"And remember you did not hear this from me."

"Thanks, you should join us...think about it," Jason casually walked back to the Youth's hang out.

Billy watched him intently, and said in a whisper, with a grin, "No, thank you."

He then strolled over to the weight-lifting area where the Brothers Inc. hung out. There was no real leader in this gang, so he just walked right into the middle of a group of them, "Wow, did somebody just turn off the lights in here?"

That got their attention and they looked at him as if he was crazy. One of the brothers approached him, "What you want cracker?"

"Hey, I've come in peace here. No need for that. I got some info I think you should have."

"Oh really? And why the fuck are you telling us for, white boy?"

"Well, just say I don't like people who don't play fair. I mean if we can't play games in peace, what else we going to do in here? What I'm getting at is, remember a couple of months ago, that little confrontation between Crusher and Roberto. I heard them talking after the game, they were going to do something about it. The subject came up again. I heard that tomorrow out on the field at 1:30 sharp they are going to take Crusher out of the game for good, if you know what I mean."

"No fucking, greasy, Mexican is going to kill me!"

"Listen to me, they do not know that I am telling you this, so play it cool and act like you don't know anything, then jump them before they have a chance to jump you."

"Oh we will! The Brothers Inc. ain't going out like no punks!"

"Just one thing. I did not tell you guys this, alright? I still have a reputation to uphold."

"Yeah, no problem, we cool. You're alright in my book, for a whitey."

"Fight the power," he raised his hand mimicking the Black Panthers. They all started to laugh, Billy walked off laughing too, but for other reasons.

He then moved over to the side of the wall, where the Cholos hung out. He met up with Paco, their head guy.

"What up, Cuz?"

"Nothing much Paco. It's always been cool between us, right?"

"Yeah, sure homes. We never had a beef with you."

"Good, because you got to trust me on what I'm going to tell you," he kneeled down next to Paco. "Well, you know how the Sing Dragons keep to themselves... I've found out why. They are planning to take control of this place. I heard them say you guys are the second biggest gang in here and you are the first ones to go."

"*¿Que?* Those fucking Chinks said that?"

"I'm afraid so. I like the way things are around here and I don't want it to change. I just found out that this is going to happen tomorrow at 1:30 sharp.

"Those fucking slant-eyes are not taking over without a fight. I promise you that."

"That's exactly what I wanted to hear."

"What did you say?"

"Oh, nothing, just remember that this info did not come from me."

"No worry, homes."

Next stop, the Sing Dragons. This would be a tough one. He had never talked to the Dragons before and he needed to find a way that he could gain their trust. They hung out at the other side of the field, next to the gated fence. They had the best spot in this place. From back there you could keep a good eye on things. They watched him as he approached from across the field, like a bunch of hungry vultures. As he reached the fence, two large Asian's blocked his path.

"What do you want here, Billy?"

"Oh, you know my name."

"Yeah, we know who you are, but not what you want."

"Well it has occurred to me that I have never met any of you guys yet. And if we are going to be here for a while I figured, what the hell. So who is in charge?"

The big guys just stood there dumfounded. Then a little Asian kid came walking between the big guys. He was five foot nothing and weighed one hundred pounds soaking wet.

"Don't mind them. They are here only for intimidation. My name is Cook."

"Ha, Can you do any? You know, cook? Ha...um...just joking."

Cook smiled politely, "So Billy, what brings you over here?"

"Like I was telling the twin towers over here. We've never met before and I was figuring it would be good to know a connection like yourself. I know you guys are from the city and I am from a small town. But one day I would like to move up and I don't want to be stepping on anybody's toes if you catch my drift."

"That is wise of you. We know of your rep and we would be honored if we could come to some kind of agreement. But I warn you, just as we know of you, you should know of us. I won't even bother telling you what we do to betrayers."

It was like he was reading Billy's mind.

Now he understood why this gang was quickly getting larger and stronger. They could see right through people. Inside he was a bit scared, but he kept his poker face on the whole time. "Come on, don't worry about that." Billy looked around and then got closer to Cook. "To prove my honesty, I'll give you some info that you can use. You know how your boy is in the hole right now?"

"Yeah, you mean Phan?"

"Some of my people overheard Mr. Bull talking to the Adolph's Youth. Seems like they are teaming up to bump you guys out of the game. Mr. Bull agreed to leave their drug business alone if they would help get you guys in trouble. Mr. Bull is trying to push for a new policy. This new rule, if the warden agrees, will go mostly against big gang populations. And right now that is you. If passed, there will be no solitary confinement. Instead, straight to prison. First, starting with your boy, Phan. And as for your gang, well you can't really defend yourselves. If a fight breaks out, Mr. Bull is going to make it your fault no matter what. Slowly your gang will get smaller and smaller. All of your tough and hardcore guys will have the same fate as Phan. Now you know how Mr. Bull has a lot of swing in here. I think this is going to happen."

Cook chuckled and looked away.

"Look. This is fucking important shit here. I'm telling you this to protect you. If I had your power, I would burn that Bull at the stake!"

Cook stared at him for a couple of seconds, and then shook his head, no. "We have nothing more to talk about," he walked off back through the two large Asians.

"Alright! It's your funeral!"

"Cook is done with you. You leave now or we'll break you!"

He looked up at the large Asians and gave them a dirty look, then flipped them off as he walked away.

Fuck! Fuck! Fuck! I don't think that he bought it. Perhaps I'll have to think of something else for the Sing Dragons.

Later that day he and Dean were sitting in their cell, booking time.

"Um, Billy I found out today that you were making the rounds to all the gangs. What's up?"

"Nothing. Just part of the plan."

"I'm not saying that your plan sucks, but, you made it pretty obvious that you are instigating whatever it is that you want them to do."

"I know. If everything goes right, it won't matter, and I

will definitely have left my mark here."

"Alright," Dean shook his head in disbelief.

"I'll tell you this, like I tell all my friends. I always come out on top. Just get Guy and the Smack Brothers out on the top of the bleachers next to the barbed wire fence tomorrow at 1:30 sharp, alright?"

"Yeah sure, no problem."

He lied back in his bunk and put his arms behind his head, and relaxed, contemplating the morrow.

Dean stared at him and wondered, *What is his big plan? How do I fit in? If at all...*

***

Day who gives a fuck,

Dear journal, this will be my last entry because tomorrow I'm getting out of this place. I did not serve my time, but I don't care anymore. I need to get out of this place and take my friends with me. Most importantly, I need to see the girl I have fallen in love with. I know she will not approve of how I'm setting this up to get out, but I need to do what I have to do. I am doing it for her. If everything works out, I'll be happy for the first time in my life.

The next morning he woke very early to watch the sunrise. He remembered a letter from Savanna, in it she described a sunrise, her words were far more beautiful than what he could see through those bars. He heard birds chirping, which broke the silence. He smiled. It was like the calm before the storm.

Suddenly, a loud horrific scream echoed throughout the facility. Everyone in the prison home sat up in their beds and listened to the torturous shrills of pain and suffering, but who was it this time? Dean looked up at Billy and saw him staring blankly out at the sun. The blood-curdling screams did not phase him at all.

"Hey Billy, are you listening to this?"

He grinned, "Yeah, I hear it."

"What, who, do you think it is?"

"It sounds like a person burning at the stake. I guess the Dragon's lit the torch."

The ear-agonizing screams eventually died.

"What? What are you talking about? Do you know who was screaming?"

"Yeah, no one we liked much."

Dean saw a look in his eyes that he had never seen before. He envisioned it as if he saw the flames of Hell reflecting from his pupils. Dean quietly laid back down, but he did not sleep. He kept one eye open, on Billy. He was scared of him, and unsure of what to expect.

In silence, he continued to watch the sunrise.

***

It was 1:25p.m. when Billy climbed to the top of the bleachers. He was holding something behind his back. Waiting there, were Dean, Guy, and the Smack Brothers.

"You guys are early. Good!" Billy looked out at the empty field.

"Billy, did you know that Mr. Bull was burnt alive this morning?"

"Really Jimmy? You don't say," he remarked coolly.

Jimmy smiled at him knowing he had something to do with it, "It must have been a beautiful sight."

Dean looked around, "This is weird! Where are all of the guards? Usually there are at least six watching over the field alone."

"You see Dean, it is standard procedure for the warden to call a meeting if a casualty among the guards occurs. Lunch time I figure, is the best time to have those meetings. Everyone should be eating and there should be no major problems. But they did forget one thing; they forgot that they have me in this place. Now they will learn the hard way, that they should never turn their backs on me."

"So, what are we doing out here?"

He put his finger up to his mouth to shush Dean. "Watch and wait."

Three minutes passed and the Youth walked onto the field from the north side. Jason and the Youth formed over fifty-plus kids. From the south end, came the Brothers Inc. They took the opposite side of the field and approached the Youth.

"What are you Honkies here for?"

"Don't act stupid, Spade. You thought that you could pull a fast one. Huh?"

"Look, you better get out of my face whitey, before I—"

"Before you what?"

Paco walked down the field and The Cholos followed closely.

"Oh here comes those wetbacks now. What you think, you can take me on?" Crusher raised his hands in the air taunting The Cholos.

"You talking to me? You feel like dying, *esé*?"

"You got a problem with the way I play football?"

"Matter of fact, if you are going to bring that up, yes I do."

"Beat it, this is between blacks and white, not brown shit!"

"You fucking Nazi fuck, I'll kill you!"

Cook and The Sing Dragons took the eastern region of the field.

"Hey Jason, yeah you, you fuck. We set a blaze to your faggot buddy."

Jason stared at him, without a clue.

"You know what I'm fucking talking about."

"Fuck you Cook. Keep your chink ass out of this!"

The four leaders of the gangs yelled back and forth at each other as the tension became thick. Almost all of the inmates were gathered on the field. The rest wanted nothing to do with the building, angry storm, they all drifted out of harm's way.

One of the guards on duty took notice and called it in, "It looks like there is going to be a riot."

Billy heard the truck pull up from behind the bleachers of the barbed-wire fence. He nodded at the driver.

Sick Boy jumped out and tied a chain around the fence

and jumped back into the truck.

Guy watched, "Hey, isn't that Sick Boy in that truck?"

The mob on the field yelled louder and emotions were running very high. Billy turned and looked at Dean, Guy, and the Smack Brothers and asked, "Are you ready to have some fun?" He held a rock, the size of a baseball behind his back that he had carefully chosen from the courtyard. He then stood like a major-leaguer in center field, cocked his throwing arm, and with all his might, he whipped that rock right into the middle of the incensed crowd. He did not care who it would hit, it didn't matter because he knew, as soon as that rock struck home, the fight would explode. Nobody knew who threw it, they just began flailing fists at anyone within reach. Total mayhem ensued.

Billy stood there in awe, watching the show, he almost did not want to leave. He wanted to watch the chaos that he created.

One of the guards doing his rounds rushed over to pull the riot bell.

He snapped out of his daze, and jumped off the bleachers, and gave Sick Boy the signal.

Sick Boy floored it, ripping down the fence.

The break-out alarm sounded but no one paid attention because the riot alarm went off at the same time. Billy jumped into the back of the truck and looked at his fellow inmates.

"Hey! Assholes! What the fuck are you waiting for?"

It took a few seconds for the shock to wear off. What had their leader just done? It happened so quick. Dean, Guy, and the Smack Brothers jumped off the bleachers and ran to the back of the moving truck, and leapt in. Billy unhooked the chain and climbed into the front seat. He leaned over and honked the horn, some of the combatants stopped fighting momentarily and took notice of the fleeing truck.

"IT'S A BREAK OUT!" Everyone made a run for it. There were not a enough guards to stop the mass of charging boys.

Billy and the boys sped down the street. He looked back at the anarchy he caused. Proud of himself, he yelled, "YEE-

HAH!"

Sick Boy loved every minute of it. He had the biggest smile on his face. As for everyone else, they were scared to death.

"Billy, man! Fuck! Oh shit! I mean, they will be looking for us, right?"

"Don't worry about it Guy! It will take them awhile before they can figure out exactly who escaped. We're not first on their list. Some major gang-bangers probably escaped, too. I figure if we lay low, that'll buy us some time."

"What happens when we run out of time?"

Billy looked back at Guy, "Where the chips fall, they fall. You're not losing faith in me, Guy, are you? You know I always come out on top."

Guy turned his head and watched the trees go by as the truck raced down the road. Guy mumbled, "Yeah! Billy comes out on top, but what about everyone else around him?"

Billy and Sick Boy talked about everything that had happened since he'd been gone. For the stunned boys in the back of the truck, the three hour ride home remained a quiet one.

CHAPTER 6

Lost and Found

They spent the next ten days surveilling Billy's house for law enforcement activity, from a distance. Knowing full well that his house would be the first place the cops would probably look. And the detectives and an occasional patrol car did make a few runs to the house, checking the empty structure for the young fugitives.

The boys managed to rough-camp in the near-by wooded areas and in other discreet spots on the fringe of the town, sight unseen. Late at night and during the very early morning hours before dawn, they would scramble and scrounge through business alleyways for food and supplies, ripping off an uncommonly unlocked house for food, cigarettes, beer, but they were smart about it, and never took too much from any one place, nor did they mess things up or damage anything. They had no desire to attract undue attention to their intrusions.

"Are you sure the cops won't come back here?" Sick Boy asked as they skulked their way closer to the house.

"Nope, I'm not sure of anything. We'll take turns standing watch when the rest of us sleep. Besides, I think it was Edgar Allan Poe who said, 'if you want to hide something, put it right out there in the open, so everybody can see it,' or some shit like that," Billy remarked.

"Did you learn that at school, sucker?" Sick Boy asked.

"No. From your, mama!"

A grimacing Sick Boy was not amused.

When they arrived at the house, it was still boarded up.

Billy told him, "Wait here for a second," he then walked up to the front door and peeked in through the cracks. He began to rip off the boards nailed to the front door and climbed in. It looked like the place had not been touched in years, his mom's last dinner was even on the kitchen table. Only the yellow police tape and a caution sign pervaded the interior of his former home. The sign read:

CRIME SCENE : DO NOT ENTER

The invasive tape hung everywhere. He walked softly to his mother's bedroom and studied the bloodstains on the floor. He turned away and closed the door, and then ran back to the truck.

"Hey Dean, you need a place to hang for awhile?"

"Yeah, I do...but what about Max and Jimmy?"

"Yeah you fuckers can stay too. Just try not to burn the house down, Jimmy."

"Not a problem, I mean you have a fireplace, right?"

Billy slapped Jimmy on the back of the head.

"Alright you bastards, wait here in the house, and keep quite. I'll be back soon."

Billy told Sick Boy to go to Hank's house and then jumped in back of the truck with Guy. Sick Boy tore off down the road.

"So Guy, how are you holding up?"

Guy took a deep breath, "I'm fine I guess, it'll just take some time," he paused for a moment, "Thank you, Billy. I hated that place and I don't think I could've handled it anymore."

"Hey, look at me Guy, what happened in that place can be just between you and me. Nobody has to know. Alright?"

"Yeah, I think it's better this way. Now let's never talk about this again."

He nodded and grabbed Guy in a headlock, messing up his hair.

They arrived at Hank's house, Sick Boy beeped the horn.

Hank came out pulling on a shirt, yelling, "Yeah! Yeah! What the fuck you honking at?"

"Hey fuck you, is that the way to greet your old friends?" Billy yelled from the back of the truck.

A surprised and delighted Hank ran over to the truck. "Oh shit, Billy! How the fuck did you pull this one off?"

"Oh, I've got my ways," he jumped out of the truck and gave Hank a big hug.

"Hey, what's up Guy?" Guy looked at Hank and cracked a little smile.

"So, how you been Hank?"

"Ah, same old shit, different day, you know."

"Yep, I know. So I got a favor to ask of you. Me, Dean and the Smack Brothers, you will meet them later, are going to hang low in my old house. But I'm out of room, so I was wondering if Guy could stay over at your house for a while. Just tell your mom that he got out early due to good behavior and he is completely rehabilitated."

"Yeah? He doesn't look rehabilitated to me."

"He's fine, he just needs some home-cooked meals."

"I'll see what I can do. Hey! We got to drink tonight and catch up."

"Maybe another night Hank. I got some things to take care of first."

"Alright then. I'll see you later. I can't believe you are standing here! You got to tell me how you got out."

"All in due time." Guy jumped off the truck and walked toward the Park.

Billy ran over to him, "Where you going Guy?"

"I'm going to find a nice box to sleep in."

"Fuck Guy! Were you not listening? You're staying at Hank's."

"Nah! I don't want to bother his parents again with the likes of me."

"What the fuck are you talking about? You've never cared before. Every time you got kicked out of your house, you stayed with Hank."

"I know, but this time it feels different."

"Listen to me. You are amongst friends now. The worst is behind us. Just take it one day at a time and you watch, by next month everything will be back to normal."

Guy managed a half-smile and walked off toward Hank's house.

Billy jumped into the front seat of the truck and they burned out of there.

"I got to get this truck home before my mom realizes that it's gone."

"What do you mean? You didn't ask your mom to borrow the truck so you can break out a good friend from jail?"

"That's funny, but seriously..."

"Yeah, no problem. Just drop me back off at my house. You know, I'm proud of you Sick Boy. You came through for me when I needed it the most. Don't think I'll forget this."

"Damn right you're not forgetting this! You owe me big time!"

"Yeah, yeah, you know if I had a sister Sick Boy, I'd let you fuck her."

They both laughed.

"It's going to be fun, with you back, Billy. You know this town hasn't been the same since you left."

"And it will never be the same now that I'm back."

They arrived back at the house, Billy jumped out of the truck. "I'll give you a call later and tell you what we're going to do."

Dean and The Smack Brothers were in the living room. Billy sat on the couch next to Dean, he breathed out a sigh of relief.

"So what's next?" Dean asked.

"Well, first we need to get some real food. No more prison or back-alley gruel for us. It is just P-B-R and Steak, all the time. After that, I thought I heard my bike calling me. She's going to need some T-L-C. Then I'm going to make a few house calls. I figure it's safe here if we don't use the front door, instead we'll climb through the back window, hopefully, we won't attract a lot of attention. Just keep the outside of the house the same and perhaps nobody will be the wiser."

Jimmy stood up and punched an open hand, "What about Bradley?"

"Oh, he will get his. But for now, let's get some R and R."

"W-w-w-hat's R and R?"

"Jimmy, please inform your brother what that means."

"It means don't talk you stupid fuck!" Jimmy scoffed.

"Th-th-th-that's it!" Max ran over and tackled Jimmy off the chair.

Billy and Dean stood up and watched them fight. They looked at each other and then jumped in. None of them could resist a good, old, friendly dog-pile fight. They were all laughing and very happy to be free. Billy rolled off of them and sat cross-legged on the floor. When the rest of them stopped play-fighting, Jimmy remained lying on the floor holding his aching genitals.

"Fuck! You dickhead! You punched my cock!" Jimmy continued to massage his penis.

"S-s-s-erves you right."

"Okay! Enough fucking around. It's getting dark. I'll go get us some food."

"Billy while you're out, can you get me a lighter?"

"Yeah, but don't set anything on fire yet, alright Jimmy?"

"It's not for me. It's for my hand."

"What's that?"

"You know, my twitch. It doesn't happen if I'm holding a lighter."

Billy nodded, stood up and left for Sgt. Liquor's. He played it very casual-like, although he did not avoid direct eye contact with the people he passed, he didn't stare or dwell on them either. He did use the back roads to avoid the heavier traffic. He did not want to take any unnecessary chances of being recognized.

When he arrived at the store, he noticed Mick had his back turned behind the counter. He snuck up to him and poked him in the back with his finger. "Alright motherfucker! This is a stick up!"

Mick turned slowly to face his adversary, "Take anything you want. Just leave me...Fuck, Billy! When are you going to grow up. You almost gave me a god damn heart attack!"

"Never!"

"So, how you been? Aren't you suppose to be in that boy's home?"

"Shit! No walls can hold me down, but if anybody asks, you didn't see me," he said with a wink.

"Little rascal! So what can I do for you?"

"Well you know someday I'm going to pay you back for all the stuff you've given me. I just need a few more things to survive. Then I will be out of your hair for good."

"It's no trouble, I can't imagine how it is for you right now. Take whatever you need."

"Thanks!" He went to the cooler and grabbed a couple twelve packs of Pabst Blue Ribbon and a lighter for the *pyro*. He popped the lid of one of the cans and drank half of it in one gulp. "AH! I needed that." He then grabbed a loaf of bread and two sticks of baloney. Macaroni and cheese, were a must take. He put down the groceries to open the door.

"Hey Billy! Remember, it's all on how you look at things. For example you probably see that beer you got there as being half-empty. Well, I would see it as half full," Mick tossed a pack of Lucky Strikes at him.

He snatched them out of the air, "Is that what you see, Mick? You know what I see? I don't care if the can is half-empty or full. I see that the can has beer in it and that's all that matters," he smiled, picked up his food, and walked out into the street.

Back at the house, everybody was already sleeping. He put down the groceries and dug out the lighter for Jimmy. He put the lighter in Jimmy's hand; to his amazement, the nervous twitching stopped. He headed to the garage. The garage door squeaked open, just enough for him to squeeze in and then he closed the door. He groped for the light switch and flipped it on. There she waited for him.

"Oh Jean, I missed you."

Oh Billy. Why did you do it?"

"Look I'm sorry the way things happened. Just got a little out of hand."

And what about the riot?

"I need to be with Savanna. I know we're meant for one other...don't look at me like that! I can't just stand by while Bradley hurts her."

What about your promise? Your last promise to your mom? You know the police are going to be looking for you soon. You fell in love with a girl that does not love you. And now you are planning to rage some war with Bradley. I hate to tell you this, but, you are losing yourself.

"What do you mean she 'does not love me,' of course she does. She tells me! Right? Fuck Jean, stop making me think. You are supposed to be glad that I'm back."

Yes, I am. But I'm worried about you. You never make little decisions, it's always big ones that affect everyone around you. And they are mostly bad decisions.

"Don't worry baby, I always come—"

I know, out on top.

The garage door squeaked open, "Are you okay, Billy?" Dean appeared in the doorway.

"Close the fucking door. Yeah, why do you ask?"

"Well, call me crazy, but I thought I heard you talking to someone."

"No, I was just singing, um, a Link Wray song."

Dean stood there, staring at him, puzzled. "Wow! That's a nice bike. What is it?"

"What is it? Man, it's only my first love, my baby, she's a 1950 Triumph Thunderbird 6-T!"

"Alright, shit man, you want me to leave you two alone?" Dean laughed. "So are you going to fix her up?"

He grabbed his tools and cleaning supplies, "Yep! And as soon as I'm done I'm going to visit somebody we both know."

"So you're going to visit Savanna, huh?"

"Yep." He started to work on the bike.

Dean continued to stare at him. Dean was not a stupid

person. He now understood the real reason Billy broke out. The smile on the love-sick teen said it all. It was not about taking the town back or being a bad-ass greaser, it was all about a girl, and that worried him. There was nothing really he could say to change Billy's mind. "I got a surprise for you."

"Oh really? I love surprises. What is it?"

Dean pulled out a plastic *Zip-loc®* bag and tossed it to him.

He caught it in mid-air. A familiar looking item, but the dried-up blood on the blade gave it away. It was his switchblade, the murder weapon. He became transfixed for just a moment and then tossed it back to Dean. "How'd you get this?" he shrugged, "Ah, you can have it Dean. Nothing but bad memories."

Dean understood. He wished Billy good luck with Savanna and went back into the house.

It was after eleven o'clock when he finished up on his bike. He opened up the garage door and started her up. The sound of Jean's motor announced that he was back.

He peeled out toward The Hills. On the way there, he passed Angel's house. He continued to ride a few blocks down, but then decided to turn around and see what she was doing.

He parked two houses away, Angel's dad knew that he was the only one who rode a motorcycle around this neighborhood. Her dad had never liked him because he always gave Pike bad ideas. Billy always joked around by giving him his own version of good advice. Pike was having problems at home because he started smoking, only to be like his idol. Billy would tell him, "Hey! If it makes you feel good. Do it! Don't let anybody tell you what to do. We are on this planet for one reason. To have fun! Don't live in denial, you will regret it later in life."

It was a bit humorous listening to him preach at Pike, and Pike would hang on every word he said. He snuck up to Angel's window and knocked softly on it.

Angel opened the curtains, her eyes were like saucers.

Billy stood there with a lit cigarette hanging out of his mouth.

She smiled and opened up the window and climbed out.

She pounced on him, and they hugged for a while.

"Oh my God! Billy! What are you doing here?"

"I couldn't handle it anymore, Angel. I needed to get out."

"Did you break out?"

He looked down at the ground and could not lie to her, "Yeah."

"Why, Billy? You know they're be looking for you."

"I know, but I got a plan."

Pike walked into her room, "Angel have you seen my grease?"

"Oh, here comes your little worshiper."

He leaned into the window, smiled, and said, "How's it going little greaser?"

Pike ran to the window. He could not contain his excitement. "Billy! Billy! How did you get out? I bet you had a great plan! Did you get into fights? How was it in there? What are you going to do about Bradley?"

"Hey! Hey! Get back in your room before I tell mom about your Playboy collection!" scolded Angel.

"Ah, man, I just wanna talk to Billy," he reluctantly turned to leave.

"Billy leaned into the window, "Don't worry Pike, we'll talk later and when I come back, I wanna see those Playboy mags."

Pike smiled and ran back to his room.

Angel slapped him across the arm.

"Ouch! What?"

"Don't encourage him," he held his arm and smiled.

"While you were gone, Pike has really gotten into Rockabilly music. He got a guitar and he's actually not that bad."

"Yeah, I know, he's a smart kid. That's why I want to sit down and talk with him. I don't want him to end up like me."

"There's nothing wrong with you, you just need some guidance. Maybe you need to look for a higher power."

"Oh fuck Angel, you're not gonna start preaching at me, are you?"

"I'm serious Billy, God was there to help me through the hard times."

"Is that a fact? I'm sorry, I've been shit, and pissed on, my whole life and there was nobody there to help me besides me, myself, and I. God? Fuck God! If there is a God, why is my mom dead?"

Angel looked down at the ground, she could not think of a response that would make any sense to him.

"The book says that when people die, God hand-picks them to go. People say, 'oh, it was her time to go,'" his sarcasm convinced her, she could not help him.

"So, even if there is a God. I don't like him. In fact, I would make a pact with the Devil, just to get even. Shit, I probably would have more fun in Hell anyway. I'm sure me and the red guy have a lot in common," he laughed. "Let me tell you this Angel, my sweet innocent, Angel. I did a lot of thinking when I was rotting away from inside. I discovered the meaning of life. It is simple quite frankly. One word— pleasure!"

Angel stood there, bewildered.

"It's true, like you said, you find happiness in God. That's your pleasure! Everything that people work for their whole lives is to earn pleasure. Things that make you happy is the meaning of a good life. Now, everyone has, of course, different pleasures. Like for me, I love to smoke, drink, ride my bike, be loud, party hard with my friends, and anything that the law calls illegal. If there was a religion that let me do whatever I want, hey, call me Father Billy. Yet there is not and I'm not going to live in denial just because it's the 'right thing' to do and everybody else is doing it."

"Are you done yet? Maybe when you grow up a little, you will see the light."

"I live for the moment. I know I'm a piece of shit and my life is in a steady decline, but I saw a turn going straight up toward happyville." He pulled out the Lucky Strike Zippo and lit up a cigarette. He held the Zippo up as if to examine it.

"I see the light."

"You *are* talking about Savanna, aren't you?"

He looked at her, disappointed, "I know the things that I do are bad, but I find pleasure in that. When I'm around Savanna, everything just feels right. I don't think of bad things, I just think about her and a new found happiness."

"You're in love with her! That is not your style."

"I know this, Angel. She's my, *Lion's Share*."

Angel looked down at the ground and laughed quietly. She mumbled, "I knew you were paying attention."

He gave her a slow, serious nod.

She looked into his eyes and understood. "I...I guess I'll see you later," Angel hugged him and then climbed back through her window.

He jumped on his bike, and roared off toward Savanna's house. He pulled up to her driveway and gassed it, the engine roared. Savanna pulled back the curtains and her eyes widened.

Billy gave her a big smile. For all the chaos and mayhem he created that day, her smile had made it all worth while.

She ran out the front door, right into his arms.

They embraced in total silence.

"Billy! Oh my God, Billy! I missed you."

"Yeah, I missed you too, Savanna.... More than you can actually imagine."

She smiled, "You probably say that to all the girls," she peered back over her shoulder. Her intuition on target, her dad peeked out of the window, watching them. "Let's take a walk down the street and talk."

She grabbed his hand as they walked to the sidewalk. He walked around her to the side of the road.

She stood still. "Why are you walking over there? Don't you want to walk next to me?"

He paused and looked around to see if anybody else was watching. He figured in the dark nobody would see him on the outer edge of the sidewalk.

"So, Billy, how did you get out?"

"Well, I'd rather not tell you because I know that you hate violence and everything. I don't want you to look down on me."

She looked deep into his eyes, "Billy, did anyone get

hurt?"

He looked down at the ground, "I don't know."

She backed away from him slowly.

He looked up, "No, wait! Don't go!"

She hastened her pace away from him.

He yelled, "I did it for you!"

She stopped. "What? Why?"

"I love you, Savanna. I really don't know how to say this. I tried writing it down, but I think in person is the best way to tell you how I've fallen in love with you. At first I didn't know what it was, but one night I had a dream, and I never dream, but this dream revealed what looked like my past love life. The last story was about us. Now I know what I've been feeling. It is love. Please, I've never loved anyone before. I needed to see you and I want to be with you."

She searched his eyes..."Wow, Billy, I don't know what to tell you. I think you're a great person, and I care for you a lot, but I don't love you like that."

"Why not? We have so much in common and we have a great time together. You're attracted to me right?"

"Attraction is not the issue. I think you are good- looking, but I look for other things in a guy."

His voice grew louder, "What? What, you want me to beat on you and treat you like shit? Then would you love me, like Bradley?"

She ran off into the wooded area behind her house.

He stood still for a moment and then slapped himself in the head. He ran after her, "No! Wait! Savanna!" He could see her in the distance running through the trees. He gained ground and finally caught up with her.

"Leave me alone!"

He held her by her arms.

She swatted at him, trying to break free. They tumbled to the ground. He rolled on top of her and pinned her wrists to the ground. "Calm down! Please, Savanna! I'm sorry! I did not mean it. I just love you, and I don't want you to be hurt by anyone."

She screamed louder, she struggled to free herself, she

wanted desperately punch him, but she couldn't. "You don't know how hard it is for me. I'm in love with an asshole. I know it, but I can't do anything about it. My father loves him. What am I supposed to do?" she sobbed.

He let go of her wrists and caressed her face, "I know the situation is bad and I want to help you see it through. Believe it or not, I can't stop thinking about you. 'Whenever you are feeling sad or blue. Just remember, I will always love you.'"

A tear rolled down her face but it did not belong to her, it belonged to him.

"I wrote that for you when I was inside, but I never had the balls to send it to you."

She wiped Billy's tears from her face. "That is the most beautiful thing anybody has ever said to me." She lifted her head off the ground, his warm tender lips on hers, chilled her to the bone; his passionate kiss deepened and penetrated her soul.

It seemed like an eternity for him. He had waited forever for that moment and he made it last as long as he could.

After the endless kiss, they laid side-by-side, looking up at the stars. Only the soothing sound of the wind could be heard, as they lay still, in silence.

"Billy, it can never work between us, we come from two different worlds. Sure we like some of the same things and I feel that I can tell you anything, but—"

"Let me work on that, Savanna. I'll do anything you ask me to."

"I don't want you to change for me. I like you the way you are. I just don't know right now. Give me some time to think and we'll talk about this some other time."

He lied there in silence. He had nothing left to say. He had just poured his heart out to her and she didn't seem to care. Of course he would never let it show on the outside. He stood up, "I understand." He then helped her up.

"You're so cool, thank you for understanding!"

He walked her back to her house and she kissed him on the cheek. He had a sad look on his face. She looked into his eyes and said three simple words, "Cheer up, Buttercup."

Those three simple words, he would never forget, and it made him happy. He watched her as she walked into the house. He then jumped on his bike and rode off into the night. During the ride home, he made a big decision; if he wanted the girl, he would have to play ball. He recalled her saying she looked for other things in guys that obviously he did not have. Find out what those things are, and he will be happy with her. He intended to be the ideal man for her. It sounded good to him, but he had no idea what he was getting himself into.

He arrived home and parked Jean in the garage. Walking through the living room, he could see that everybody had crashed out. He grabbed a beer and headed to his bedroom. He laid down and lit a cigarette. Staring at the ceiling he thought, *Okay she does not like violence, born with a silver spoon, so she likes guys with money. Um, fuck, what else?* After a few minutes he became frustrated. He slammed his fists on the bed, and stood up and stomped over to Dean, snoring like a locomotive.

"Wake up! Dean!"

"What? What's going on? Fuck Billy, is this going to be a habit?"

"I'm sorry, I need four-one-one about Savanna."

"What's the matter, it didn't go the way you wanted it to?" Dean rolled over and closed his eyes.

Billy grabbed him by the shoulder and ripped his attention back. "Fuck Dean, this is serious!"

Dean sat straight up. "Okay! Fuck, Billy, Jesus...look, forget about her. That chick is weird, a lost cause. It's not worth it man. Let me tell you this, the little friends that she does have, tried to help her. Shit, I tried, but she doesn't listen. The worst part is, most people live and learn, but she lives and suffers. I think she has a split personality or something. She will say one thing and do another, completely opposite from each other. Then when she does make a decision, it is still fifty-percent, so she can go back to the other one. I don't know if this is making any sense to you because you look like you're not hearing what I'm saying."

"Oh...what was that, Dean?"

"Never mind! I see that you're not even listening to me. You will learn the hard way." Dean laid back down, wanting nothing more than to go back to sleep.

"Fuck, man! You didn't tell me anything."

Dean sprang back up, "I don't know! Um, she's a plant-eater."

"You mean a vegetarian?"

"Yeah! Now leave me alone. I'm trying to sleep here."

Billy stood up and went back to his room. He laid down to try and sleep, but lied awake most of the night thinking about Savanna.

The next morning, the sounds of a squabble woke him from a light sleep. He stumbled out of bed to investigate. It was the Smack Brothers fighting over a piece of baloney. "Hey, what the fuck you guys yelling about?"

Jimmy said, "Dickhead Max over here ate most of the baloney and I'm not going to let him eat the last piece."

The Smacks continued to push each other.

"What? You ate all the fucking baloney dude? Nah! That ain't possible. Did you check the other bag Jimmy?"

"No!" Jimmy struggled as Max put him into a headlock.

"Well idiot, there should be some more in the other bag. Where's Dean?"

The boys stopped fighting.

"He sai-d-d s-s-something about b-b-bing hor-hor-ny and is going to h-h-h-hang around the highs-s-school."

"Yeah he said high school, but I'm sure he meant intermediate school."

"Shit, knowing that sick fuck, he's probably at the elementary school," Billy opined.

As depraved as the thought was, it caused them to laugh.

Billy suddenly stopped laughing, "Shut up!"

They went silent as he put his finger up to his mouth. He had heard noises outside.

The Smack Brothers heard it too. It sounded like someone was circling the house. The front door squeaked open and the Smack Brothers snuck back into the living room and stood in the doorway, waiting to grab and beat whoever would walk through.

Billy picked up a 2x4 lying on the floor and assumed an attack posture. The floorboards creaked as the footsteps got closer. He watched a shadow grow in the doorway. He raised the 2x4 higher, ready to strike...

"Billy?...Billy?"

Jesus! Pike came into view. He put down the board and motioned to the Smack Brothers that it was alright.

"Who the fuck is this kid, and how did he find us?"

"Not g-g-good"

"Pike, what are you doing here? Shouldn't you be in school?"

"Fuck school! You never went Billy, and you've turned out just fine or should I say, out on top."

Billy rolled his eyes and drew a heavy sigh.

"Jimmy, Max, look around to check if anybody followed him. Pike, come with me into the kitchen."

Pike followed his idol and sat down at the table. Billy opened the refrigerator and grabbed a beer, then tossed it to Pike. He grabbed one for himself and sat down across from Pike at the dinner table.

"Don't tell your sister I gave you a beer. She will kill me. I'm giving it to you because I know your dad will never share a beer with you and have a heart-to-heart."

Pike opened his can and guzzled a swig. He put the beer down and pretended to enjoy it, all the while, attempting to hide the fact that he could not understand why anyone would ever want to drink something that tasted so awful.

"So, how does it taste, Pike?"

"Um...damn good!"

Billy laughed, "No it doesn't. Beer, the first time, is horrible. It is a taste that you acquire over time. Then you begin to like it, then eventually, you may love it. What I'm trying to say Pike, I'm not a good role model for you. I have not chosen this hand I'm holding, I'm just playing the cards I've been dealt. I've become accustomed to my life, and now I love it. You, on the other hand, have been dealt a different hand. Fuck, you're not even playing the same game as me. Your sister told me that you have natural talent with the guitar. You can still be a bad motherfucker, but in a different way. A different game. Take that guitar, learn it, rip it, and play music that will scare the hell out of people...make them *not* forget... You know what I'm saying?"

Pike looked into his concerned eyes and sensed his sincerity. He nodded. The young, inexperienced teen understood his icon.

"I'm a fuck up! I have nothing to offer this world, but I don't care, and, I never will. That is me though. You've got something more, special. Play your cards close to the vest, and come out a winner. Don't be like me!"

Pike sniffled and rubbed his nose. He understood, but it was hard to listen to, and take to heart. It was like telling a six year old that Santa Clause is not real. After a minute of sniffling, Pike smiled and pulled two Playboy magazines out of his hip pocket, and waved them around.

Billy grinned, reached out and messed up the kid's hair.

"Don't worry Billy, Pike *will* come out on top," Pike smiled, and gave him the magazines.

"I'll be right back," he went to his room and came out carrying his guitar and amplifier. "I want you to have this Pike."

Pike's eyes lit up with excitement, "Your guitar, Billy?"

"Yeah, I'm not that good at it. Maybe you should make it wail, and grab people."

Pike accepted the vintage Fender Stratocaster from him and began to play sweet, raw licks. His natural ability flowed from his fingers and out the instrument.

Billy lit a cigarette and sat down. Pike played away in total bliss as Billy sat there listening to the burgeoning virtuoso's chops; smoking, and thumbing through the Playboys.

The back kitchen window opened and Dean climbed through. He tripped and sprawled face first to the floor. He stood up with a huge smile across his face. "Yep, yep, yep, yep, ah, oh, ah, yeah."

"Are you okay there, Dean?"

"Oh yeah, never better. Just got me some sixteen-year-old

poon-tang."

"That's great there. You know we're trying to keep a low profile, right?"

"I'm sorry, but I have to let the little girlies know that Mr. Dean is in town."

Billy shook his head. Pike continued to play the guitar.

"Oh Yeah! I also bumped into your little girlfriend too. I got some good news, she's going away on vacation with her family. She'll be gone for about three weeks. Now is the time to get your head back together and to have some fun."

"Yeah, maybe you're right, this hiding thing, fucking sucks. Our cover is going to get blown anyway, sooner or later. Little Pike here found us. Might as well live it up now. Tonight is going to be the beginning, by showing this town Billy and The Click are back and Hell has no bounds."

"That's what I'm talking about, man!" Dean raised his fist.

"Later tonight we are going to have a blast. Just like old times!" his nefarious grin lit up his face.

CHAPTER 7

The Boys Are Back

Night had fallen and Billy decided to get everyone together at his house. With no phone, Billy sent the Smack Brothers to get Sick Boy, and Dean, and then to fetch Hank and Guy. He sat in the living room alone smoking a cigarette, waiting for everyone to return. Half an hour later, he heard loud voices approaching. He walked to the back door to greet his friends. First came Hank and a boy with a blue mohawk who looked somewhat familiar.

"Hey, how's it going Billy? I brought Doug over! You remember Doug, right?"

Doug, was a local kid, big into the punk scene. He never said much of anything. Billy remembered seeing him around town but had never really met him before now.

Doug had a twelve pack of Pabst Blue Ribbon.

"Hey, anyone who's a friend of Pabst is a friend of mine." Billy smiled and shook his hand.

Guy walked in accompanied by a known drug-dealer named, Fool. This kid was a total joker. He had done so many drugs in his life that he had lost his common sense, furthermore, he had a reputation for doing anything, just for a laugh. Billy didn't care because he knew Fool could supply the party.

"What's going on Guy?"

"Nothing but the rent. Oh, and I brought over Mr. Happy."

He stared at Fool, "You must be Mr. Happy."

"Yep! But you can just call me Mister!"

Billy pushed him into the house, "Get the fuck out of here."

Fool smiled and laughed, as he strutted into the living room.

Dean followed close behind, with two chicks under each arm and three more girls trailing behind him.

"I see you brought some lovely young ladies tonight Dean."

"Oh, I want you to meet the *slut sisters* here under my arms and the *high school whores* behind me."

Dean's bluntness while in the presence of the girls shocked him. The girls seemed undaunted by the crude comments, giggling as they sauntered by.

Stupid girls, Billy thought. It seemed, while they were with Dean, they were willing to throw their dignity out the window.

Sick Boy and the Smack Brothers were the next to arrive.

"Billy! So, what are we doing tonight, come on! Tell me!" Sick Boy was itching to raise some hell.

"Calm the fuck down. Didn't you listen to the weather channel? It said there is a strong possibility of snow, if you get my drift."

Sick Boy smiled and walked in.

"Jimmy, Max! Are you guys gonna come in or you gonna stand there and wait for a fucking invitation?"

"Yeah, we're coming in. We're just distancing ourselves from that lunatic, Sick Boy."

"What do you mean?"

"On the way here he was yelling at all the cars that passed us. He threatened to kick their asses if they got outta their cars."

"Yeah, well, he can be somewhat improper at times."

Jimmy walked into the house shaking his head, sparking up his precious lighter. Max followed close behind.

Billy shut the door and walked into the living room which had now become a rollicking party. One of the girls brought a stereo, cool Rockabilly music pulsated. Billy stood on top of the coffee table and told them, to lower the volume.

"Okay, listen up fuckers. Tonight is the beginning of a new era for this town. An era where it will be cool to be a punk or a greaser, hell, even a skinhead. An era where the night will be ruled by the walking dead, and jocks will have to be checking in early. We start tonight, we will make it known to all in this town that we, The Click, are back and badder then ever!"

Everyone grabbed their beer cans and raised them high, yelling and shouting. The music cranked back up and Billy leaped off the table.

After an hour of hard partying everyone was pretty well wasted. Fool had supplied everyone with more than enough drugs and booze. They all were giddy, and having a great time.

Sick Boy, lounged on the sofa, engaed in an intense conversation with Max. Billy decided to cruise over and join in.

"Listen to me Max. It's called chicken fuck."

"I don't kn-kn-know, it-it sounds cr-cr-crazy."

"What are you guys talking about?" asked Billy.

Sick Boy asked, "You heard of chicken fucking, right?"

"Yeah, yeah that's what your dad does when your mother ain't home."

"No, serious Billy, you don't know?"

He just shook his head.

"You need three people. One guy holds a girl down while the other guy fucks her. When you are about to cum, the third guy takes out a knife and slits the girls neck. The body will go into convulsions and for the guy fucking her, the feeling is suppose to be so intense, it will be the best fuck you've ever had."

Max and Billy stared at him in amazement. Max then got up and walked away.

"What, are you fucking nuts? That is the most fucked up thing I've ever heard in my life. Sick Boy, you need some help," Billy said as he walked away from the sick fuck too.

"Pussies! You're just fucking scared, that's all! Come on, I need someone to hold a bitch down! Who's with me?"

Billy sat down in an over-stuffed recliner across the room trying to get that creepy image out of his head. One of the girls, eyed him, and decided to move in. She sat down on his lap and put her arms around his neck.

"Hello Billy, my name's Candy."

"Really?"

"I heard so much about you. I can't believe that I'm actually talking to you."

"Yeah, well you'll get over it. How old are you?" She looked very young and knowing Dean's taste, she probably had seventh grade homework to turn in tomorrow.

"Fifteen. Why? How old are you?"

"Shit, honey, I'm an old man. You know, the Dead Sea. I'm so old I remember when it was sick!"

She laughed and put her hand on his crotch.

"You're so funny. Let's go to your room." She continued to caress his groin.

A drunken Billy blurted, "Good God, this girl is easy."

She did not care though. She just giggled, grabbed his hands, pulled him to his feet, and lead him toward the bedroom. They passed Dean on the way.

"Tell me how she is, because I got seconds."

He smiled as he disappeared into the bedroom with Ms. Easy.

Guy, Jimmy, Max, Doug, Fool, Hank and the *slut sisters* gathered around a table and played an intense game of Quarters.

During Fool's second shot he wanted to make a new rule so he took his sweet time.

"Would you hurry the fuck up and shoot already?" Hank slapped him on the back.

"Hey, don't fuck up my concentration," Fool cautioned.

"Fuck Fool! Shoot!" said Jimmy.

Soon everyone was complaining.

He finally shot and it went straight into the glass.

"Bam! See, just for making me rush, the rule is going to be...every time one of you bitches swear, you have to drink!"

"Ah, fuck that!" said Doug.

"AH! AH! You got to drink!" said Fool, with a big smile.

"Ah shit, I forgot."

"Oh, and one more too!" They all laughed at Doug.

Doug guzzled his drink, and then a second. He slammed the can on the table and looked at Fool.

"Fuck You!" Doug fell off his chair and passed out.

"Well, Doug's out," Fool announced.

Everyone roared.

Jimmy and Max walked over to Dean. He had the two young girls all over him.

"Hey Dean, come here for a second," requested Jimmy.

"Excuse me ladies, I'll be right back," he strolled over to the Smack Brothers. "What the fuck you guys want? I'm getting my quality time in here."

"Yeah, we know that. But fuck Dean, you know we've been in prison too. I just want to wet my pickle also. And I'm speaking for Max too."

"Yeah, w-w-wet pickle."

"Oh I see, you want me to share, and share alike, right? I don't know Jimmy. I don't think they would like your style. The whole *ugly* thing ain't working out for you," Dean laughed. "Nah! just fucking with you. Which one you want?"

"I like th-th-the b-b-blonde."

"Yeah, I like that one too, that's why you're taking the brunette. It doesn't matter it's all pink and wet from the inside, right?"

Dean rejoined the girls, "I got a favor to ask of you, Jessica."

"My name is Amy."

"Whatever. You see my friend over there?"

"The one with the scar on his face?" Amy pointed at Jimmy.

"No, he's second." Dean pointed at Max, who was practically drooling, "The big idiot-looking one over there."

"Yeah," Amy replied nervously.

"He's been in prison for a while and he lacks much needed comfort from a sweet young thing like yourself."

"What are you getting at? You want me to go over there and suck him dry and then after that fuck scarface 'till he blacks out?"

"Um, I couldn't say it any better."

"Sure, anything for you, Dean."

Amy sashayed over and grabbed Max and led him toward the bathroom.

Dean went back to what he was doing before being rudely interrupted.

Meanwhile in Billy's room, some heavy making-out steamed up the bed. She moaned as he put his hand down her panties. She was almost naked when he suddenly stopped. That ruined the moment.

"What's the matter, Billy? Am I not everything you want?" She caressed her naked breasts and stomach.

He looked her in the eye and said, "Well...no, you're not!"

Furious, a humiliated Candy scrambled to her feet and put her clothes on and ran out of the room.

He laid back and lit up a cigarette. He just couldn't do it. The old Billy would have, in a heartbeat, but, he was in love and he could not stop thinking about Savanna. He smiled as he took a another drag on the cigarette. He then went back into the living room.

"Dude, what happened? She took off running," Dean asked.

"Oh you know, I busted out the monster and she got scared, took off runnin'. Stupid high school chicks. Doesn't matter, we got better things to do. Let's go fuck-up this town!" he yelled as he ran out the door.

The gang cheered and trailed after him. They all jumped into their cars.

The bathroom door swung open and Max ran out with his pants down at his ankles. "Hey! w-w-where are you g-g-guys g-g-going?" Max shouted as he watched the vehicles peel out down the street. Max pulled up his pants and staggered back into the house.

It was midnight. They raced down the street at speeds up to one hundred and ten miles per hour. Billy was behind the wheel of a cherry '57 Chevy with Guy, Fool, Jimmy, and the girls who owned it.

Hank sat at the wheel of a sweet 1965 G.T.O. with Dean, Doug, and the rest of the girls in the backseat.

They all pulled up to a street light. It was red and they began to rev the engines. The girls in back were yelling for more. Fool was flipping off Hank, who then looked over at Billy and saw that grin and a green sparkle in his eye. Before he knew it, Billy scorched rubber.

"Oh shit!" Hank punched it.

Billy had a huge lead and he scanned ahead for on-coming traffic. Weaving in and out, he avoided the cars in his path, but Hank still gained ground.

"Fucking move!" Billy yelled. But the pedal was jammed to the floorboards.

Hank caught up and they were neck and neck. Their intense expressions matched their determination. Everyone in Billy's car was chanting, "Billy! Billy!" Up ahead, two semi-trucks were blocking the road. There was a narrow path through the trucks, but only one car would be able to squeeze through. The dueling vehicles screamed down the road. They hit one hundred and twenty miles per hour, closer and closer they drew to the semi-trucks.

Billy let out a banshee yell and cut Hank off, sending him into a spin. He then ripped right through the semis and pulled out in front of the startled truck drivers. Not a scratch. Out of the rear-view mirror he saw that Hank had slid out of control onto side of the road. The passengers looked on, stunned and shocked.

"Now that's what I call a fucking race!" A wild-eyed Billy bantered. He pulled up to the bar, Outsiders. He climbed out and lit up a cigarette. About five minutes later Hank pulled up.

"Fucking Billy! You almost made me slam into the fucking trucks!"

Billy grinned, "But you didn't, right? I told you boy, you mess with the bull, you get the horns."

Hank stared enviously and then smiled. He could never stay angry at his best friend for very long. He just had that personality that you loved to hate, and respect.

All the passengers got out of their cars and stormed into the bar, following their leader.

The bar patrons stopped what they were doing and stared at Billy and The Click. The black-leather jacketed Click stood their grinning back at them. The patrons then turned their attention back on their own activities and conversations.

Billy strutted on in and over to the bar. The Click strolled to the back wall of the bar, to their usual table, to find some new cats sitting there.

Hank, Sick Boy, Jimmy, and Guy confronted them.

"Hey! I know you guys are new here because you're in our seats, at our table," Hank exclaimed ever so politely.

"Yeah! We're going to ask you nicely and only—" Jimmy began.

"So get the fuck out of our seats before I tear you a new asshole!" Sick Boy threatened.

The head of the gang stood up, "I don't see a name on this table."

Hank sneered and pushed the gang's beers off the table. The bottles splattered to the floor. He then drew their attention to a spot on the table.

There, carved deep into the tabletop; 'BILLY.' The gang may have been new, but they were not stupid, they knew his reputation, and that of The Click.

"Oh! Shit! I'm sorry, I didn't know. Billy's not here? Is he?" asked one of the dudes sitting at the table.

Hank pointed at him sitting at the bar, talking to the bartender. The new gang got up and went over to the bar to pay their respects.

"Um, Bartender, can you give a round of beers to Billy here, and his friends over there," requested the sheepish leader.

Billy turned around to identify his new, generous host.

"I'm sorry Billy, I didn't know. I hope this will bury the hatchet."

He gazed back at the Click's table somewhat puzzled.

Hank gave Billy an 'OK' sign with a smile.

He looked again at the dude and smiled.

"You know they're just fucking with you. You don't have to buy us drinks."

"Oh! But I want to."

Billy winked at the bartender, "Alright, it's your dime. A round of gin and tonics."

"Sure," Todd, the bartender mixed and served the drinks.

"Hey, Billy, get the fuck over here!" yelled Hank.

He grabbed his fresh drink and headed over to the table.

"Fuck Billy, our first night out and you're hanging out at the bar. Come on! Hang with the boys."

He sat down and the whole Click joined in at the table. A punk band was playing that night, so it was a rough crowd. Everyone in the place was blitzed. Guy turned and whispered something to Fool. Guy then looked at Sick Boy, Hank, and Billy, then smiled. Dean looked pretty comfortable with the two girls under his arms. They all knew what was going on. Fool had two bags of coke left. Not enough to go around, and like Billy always used to say, "sharing does not mean caring." The five stood up and made their way to the bathroom.

Jimmy asked, "Dean, I wonder how my brother's doing? Dean! Hey! You listening to me?"

Dean pried his lips off one of the girls, "Don't worry about him. He's in good hands." He turned his attention back to the girls and groped both of them.

In the bathroom, high as kites, the boys snorted their lines.

Meanwhile, outside the bar, a couple of police cars pulled up quietly into the parking lot. The cops scoped out the girl's cars. They received citizen complaints about vehicles racing down the street and driving recklessly.

Through the bar door, walked three cops. It was Lt. Gip, Detective O'Neil, and one other officer. They stormed up to the bartender.

O'Neil showed Todd a mug shot of Billy. "Have you seen this kid? He broke out of a boy's home awhile back."

Todd glimpsed at the photo and nodded no.

"How about this kid? His name is Kelly, but he goes by

Sick Boy." Gip demanded, thrusting the mugshot at Todd.

Todd looked up briefly at the photos and then went back to wiping down washed glasses.

An angered Lt. Gip pushed O'Neil to the side and grabbed Todd by the collar and growled, "I know that fucker hangs out here and it was him drag-racing down the street tonight! I got enough dirt on this place to shut it down for good. Just tell me where he's at and I will have a sudden case of amnesia about the shit that does go down in this place."

Todd thought for a couple of seconds, and then reluctantly pointed at the men's room door.

The lieutenant released his grip on Todd and walked toward the men's room.

Todd called out to the lieutenant. "I almost forgot to tell you about the secret knock. Knock three times, then slowly twice."

The lieutenant grinned, pulled his .45, and cautiously approached the rest room.

Todd grinned, and grabbed his baseball bat and prepared himself for whatever would happen next.

The cops passed Dean and Jimmy on the way there, but ignored them.

On the other hand, Dean paid attention while the officers moved toward the men's room. He told the girls to smother him so he would have cover. Under the table he pulled out the switch blade and readied himself for the worst. He kicked Jimmy from under the table then nodded in the direction of the men's room door.

Jimmy looked up and clinched his lighter tight in his fist.

The band continued to play, oblivious to the impending chaos.

Gip leaned against the door and listened. He knocked three times slowly.

"Shhh! Did you hear that?"

"What? I didn't hear anything."

"Yeah! I heard it," said Guy.

"It sounds like someone is knocking on the door," Fool

said.

Three more slow knocks on the door.

"I don't like this, nobody knocks on doors around here," Billy put his ear to the door and heard whispers. He stepped back and raised his left foot. With all his might he kicked the door open. It slammed into the lieutenant's face and the large cop reeled backward onto a table. Drinks flew everywhere.

Billy stood there, looking down on the sprawled out lieutenant. The ruckus caused isolated fights to break out, and then the whole place erupted. Beer bottles zipped through the air like missiles, crashing into bodies, and walls. The screaming could be heard in the street.

Billy barked, "It's time to go! Out the window!" He then jetted through it. The Click and some of the patrons were right behind him.

Lt. Gip fought his way through the crowd out to the parking lot. A few stray fists crashed into his jaw, chest, and shoulders for his trouble. He remained determined to finish his fight through the pandemonium.

Dean and Jimmy rushed the embattled lieutenant. Jimmy pounced on him from behind and held his arms. Gip twisted and squirmed attempting to free himself.

Dean jumped in front of the struggling cop, "Hey, remember me? Tell your daughter, Dean's back in town, motherfucker!"

His knife plunged repeatedly into the lieutenant's stomach like a runaway piston. Gip crumpled to the ground in excruciating pain. His fellow officers ran to aid their seriously wounded comrade.

Dean and Jimmy ran for it. Jimmy made it, but Dean tripped and fell. Two of the officers caught up to him and pounced. They pressed him down and the three rolled around in the sweat, the beer, the broken glass, and blood.

Billy and The Click hustled to one of the cars. They piled in and screeched out of there in a smoky cloud of burnt rubber.

A stampeding Jimmy, burst through the front door and stumbled onto the ground. He ran hard after the speeding car carrying his friends away.

"Slow down! Jimmy is right behind us," Hank shouted.

Billy peered into the rear-view mirror. "Damn that boy's quick. Let's see if he can catch up," he laughed.

"Yeah! I got five bucks on him," a giddy Sick Boy said.

"Oh, you guys are fucked up. But I'll take that bet," Hank said.

A shocked Fool and Guy sat in the backseat, disapproving of the bet.

Jimmy ran for his life, "Stop! You fuckers!"

Sick Boy screamed, "Come on Jimmy, you can do it!"

"No Jimmy, slow down we'll turn around and pick you up!" Hank cautioned.

Billy saw fear in Jimmy's eyes, he slowed down. The front door swung open and Jimmy dove in.

"That was an easy five dollars."

"Bullshit! I ain't paying you shit, Sick Boy."

An out of breath Jimmy said, "You dick! Didn't you see me? And you two fuckers...are betting on me!"

Hank and Sick Boy laughed.

"Real fucking funny. You know fucking Dean is still back there! He fucking stabbed the lieutenant with that god-damn knife!"

"Don't worry! Dean's a big boy, he can take care of himself."

"I can't believe those *pigs* are on me already," Billy mumbled to himself.

"Hey Billy, it's been real, but I see you guys are in some major shit so you can just drop me off at the next corner."

Disturbed by his cowardice, he shot Fool a look of disapproval, and then slammed on the brakes.

"Alright, puss! Get the fuck out then!"

Fool got out, and before he could close the door, Billy peeled out.

"What arc wc going to do?" asked Hank.

He did not say anything for awhile, then he blurted, "I don't know, we'll see where the chips fall. But for right now let's get Max and we'll go from there."

They pulled up in front of the eerily quiet house. The front door was wide open. They all jumped out and skulked their way in, cautiously. The interior had been trashed. It looked like a tornado had hit it.

Max was nowhere to be found. Jimmy yelled for his brother. They checked all the rooms but still, no Max.

Hank went to the bathroom to take a piss. A motionless, bloody Max laid sprawled and twisted across the toilet and floor. He was dead. Hank hung his head, "Oh shit," he said under his breath. Hank wobbled back into the living room, dazed, "uhm, Billy, I think you should see this."

He sensed the grave urgency in Hank's eyes and shaky voice.

Discovering Max's contorted, bloody flesh, freaked Billy out. He unwillingly flashed back on his mother's death. "No! This can't be!" He kneeled down next to Max.

Jimmy ran into the bathroom, his face flushed, and his heart pounded as he looked in disbelief at his brother's lifeless body. He pushed Billy out of the way. Tears streamed down his face as he gently cradled Max's bloodied head in his arms and rocked him. "What going on? What's wrong with him? He can't be.... He's all I've got left!.... He's all I got! He sobbed uncontrollably, pressing his face into his brothers chest, rocking back and forth. His unconsolable distress then turned to rage and hate, "Who the fuck did this?"

Billy stood up and looked into the mirror.

Scribbled in blood, the message read:

"WE SILENCED THE RETARD!"

"Bradley." Billy dead-panned. His fist crashed into the mirror, slivers and shards flew everywhere.

CHAPTER 8

Rumble

The next couple of weeks were quiet. Although to Billy, it felt like the calm before the storm. To everyone else concerned, it was a different story. They all knew that Max's death would be avenged. A full-fledged war had begun between The Click and Bradley's thugs. The Click's messengers met resistance and fights broke out all over town.

Fires were set and burned out of control keeping the authorities busy. Jimmy. The flames of Hell in his heart, "Fire it up!" his battle cry.

All of the boys struggled with their inner demons that churned and ate at their embattled souls.

The word on the street said an on-the-mend Lt. Gip had been tipped-off by Bradley that Billy, and The Click were responsible for the riot at the bar and that Dean had stabbed Lt. Gip who was still 'officially' listed in 'critical condition' at the local hospital. Dean disappeared and no one had heard from him since. The cop shop had put out an ATL for him.

He sat in his house days on end, alone. Drinking and thinking about how things could have been different. Savanna returned to town two days prior, but a cautious Billy could not bring himself to go see her. He knew it probably would be pointless. The girl he loved could not care less about him and when she found out about Dean and the street war, he would be number one on her shit list, a real downer for him. He drank heavily, he would stop only when he passed out in a stupor.

A knock on the front door stirred the groggy teen from his drunken sleep. He stumbled to the door and peeked out the make-shift eyehole to spy who was there; Angel. "Go around back," he slurred and spit.

He fumbled with the back door lock before managing to open it.

"Billy you look like shit. Where have you been for the last couple weeks?" Angel stared into purple, sunken, blood-shot eyes.

"I've been thinking."

"You know this town's been crazy while you've been *thinking*, the police can't stop all the fights. There are fires so out of control that the fire department can't handle all of them, and it seems like everyone is crazy. It's total anarchy!"

He relished the thought and mumbled, "At least The Click is having fun."

"I heard about this huge rumble that will finish everything."

"Yeah, I heard about that too. It's Sick Boy's idea."

"Billy! What are you doing? Call off this rumble! You can stay at my place and get back on track."

"Yeah sure, your dad is going to love that one. Forget about me Angel, I'm a lost cause."

"Why do you think like that?"

"I wish I could think otherwise. But it seems like every move I make, it ends up to be the wrong one. I'm cursed!"

Angel looked down and shook her head in disbelief.

"Remember when I told you Angel, that I don't believe in God. Well, now I do, and he's out to fuck my life up."

"Oh Billy, what's become of you?"

He squinted as he lit up a cigarette.

It was tearing her apart inside, she could not do anything for him. She moved in close, and kissed him on the lips. No reaction. Dejected, Angel looked deep into his eyes and then turned away and walked out of his life, probably forever.

She headed toward The Hills, deep in thought, *What am*

I going to do about him? What can I do to help him? She thought how she loved him so very much, more than enough to give him up, and walk away. As painful as that could be for her, she knew that it could never work between them. She walked on, examining her feelings and thinking everything out. She blurted, "My God, he is so, impossible!" The rumble of an approaching vehicle behind her interrupted her thoughts. The car ripped by her, and then skidded to a halt a few houses down. Angel drew closer and could hear elevated voices.

Savanna popped out of the car. She seemed very agitated. As the car pulled away, the driver yelled, "Stay away from him, I mean it, bitch!" The car ripped around the corner and disappeared.

Savanna screamed back, "Fuck off! I do what I want!"

"You're, Savanna right? Are you okay?"

"Who are you? What do you want?" her mascara had run free down her face.

Angel took a good look at her from head to toe. "Hey listen girly, let's get this straight, I don't like you, but I care about Billy. Personally, I don't see what he sees in you. All I know is that he is madly in love with you. You need to figure out what to do because it is tearing him apart."

Savanna looked away. "I know. I want to...but—"

"But what? Billy is a great guy, sure he's a little rough around the edges."

"Why don't you just date him then?" Savanna suggested, drenched in sarcasm.

"I've tried, but, Billy's in love with *you,* and I've never seen him *that* happy before. I don't want to come between his happiness. He *deserves* to be happy!"

"What am I suppose to do about Bradley? I mean I just can't leave him."

"Come on now. I'm not saying I know you or him, but from what I've just seen, I believe the stories. That relationship is not gonna work. I've never seen such a jerk in all my life, he even looks like an asshole! All I'm saying is, Billy needs you. At least go and see him at his house."

She had thought hard about Billy, and the things he had done for her. She nodded. "Yeah, maybe I should give it a try. Thanks! I didn't catch your name?"

"Well, you can call me, Angel."

"Angel? That sounds appropriate for you. Maybe we can be friends?" she suggested.

Angel leered coldly at her, "No, that won't be happening any time soon. Bye."

Savanna stood dumfounded, "Oh, Okay." *She doesn't give a shit?* Savannah continued home, and then soaked in a long, warm, soothing bath.

Three hours later she was ready to go. She looked hot, but she was not dressed for the occasion. The wind had picked up and the temperature dipped. Her dress flapped around, goose bumps covered her body as she shivered her way to his door.

"Go away Angel! Just let me die in peace!" He threw an empty beer bottle at the door.

"Um, Billy, is that you?"

He sat up, and sobered. He recognized the sweet voice. He peered through the door cracks. The most beautiful girl in the world stood there. He ripped down the boards and the door fell open.

"Hey you," she said softly.

"S-S-Savanna? Wow! Come in, come in," he sheepishly invited her in, out of the cold. Embarrassed by the disasterous mess throughout the house, he began picking up empty beer and liquor bottles, some of them were encrusted with dried vomit. Smelly pizza boxes, and pieces of pepperoni were strewn all about the living room.

"So, how have you been, Billy?"

"Oh! Um, fine. Yourself?"

"Things are good, I guess," she stretched her skirt down, trying to hide fresh bruises on her legs.

He just stared at her.

"I've missed you, Savanna," he reached for her hand.

"Yeah, I missed the fun we had," she put her hand on top of his thigh. They sat down and she rested her head on his shoulder. He put his arm around her, they sat in silence for awhile.

"I met your little friend, Angel. She's kinda weird."

"Yeah, Angel gets that way sometimes."

"No! No, not in a bad way. She actually gave me some good advice."

"Oh no, what did she tell you?"

"She thinks we should run off into the sunset together and live happily ever after. God, wouldn't that be nice? *Happily ever after?*"

"Savanna, I've got something I need to tell you."

"What is it?"

He stood up and paced up and down. "Well me and the boys were drinking at Outsiders and having a good time and everything....The fucking pigs showed up because your boyfriend ratted on us. A big fight broke out and Dean stabbed a cop. And now he's disappeared. He's on the run. The worst thing is the fucking cop survived, but, if they catch him, they'll still fry him."

She looked away for a moment. Disappointment filled her heart as she then searched his eyes for answers.

"Why, Billy, do I think there is more to this story?"

"One of Bradley's boy's killed my friend, Max. There is going to be a rumble. Not just any old cat-fight, this one will set the record straight on who owns this town. Greasers versus Preps. People are going to get hurt, maybe even die."

She sprang to her feet, "No! No! Billy! Why? Why all this macho bullshit? So what if you beat up Bradley or he beats you up? What does that prove? There is too much violence in this world all ready. Why add to it?"

He smiled at her. "That's what I love about you, Savanna. You're so innocent, oblivious to what's going on around you."

"Billy, look at me. Do you really want this to happen? Do you?"

He paced around the room some more. He then rubbed his forehead, and plopped back down and stared blankly into her eyes. "It's all I know."

"Well, learn something different. Let's do it! Let's run

away together and leave this crap behind us."

"Does that mean you want to be with, me?"

"I don't know, let's find out, just go with the flow."

He smiled and hugged her tight, lifting her off the floor.

"My dad has a cabin out in the country on a lake, it's real peaceful out there. The only problem is getting there."

"No problem. I've got my bike."

"Oh yeah, Jean, right?"

"You remembered her name?"

"Of course I did, silly."

"Okay how about, you go back to your house and pack a bag. I will meet you there in an hour. Then we will go far away from this place. How does that sound?"

"It sounds perfect."

She gave him a big hug and a peck on the cheek, then headed for the door. "Oh I almost forgot, this came in the mail for you, but it has my address on it."

He gazed befuddled, as she handed him the package.

"Bye! I'll see you in an hour, honey."

He smiled warmly at her. He thought, *Honey, huh?* He sat down and opened the package. It was stuffed with newspaper. He dug through the mass of crumpled papers and found the switch-blade, and a letter.

Billy,

Hey man, how's it going? I know you're probably wondering where the fuck I am. I figured I should split town. The pigs are not going to forget this one. You're right about this knife, it's bad news, but I heard something about it. I have no time to stop and check it out. I know I'm a wanted man right now. Take this knife to an antique shop and you should be pleasantly surprised. Take care of Savanna. She's a good girl, and she deserves to be treat-ed well. Maybe someday our paths will cross again, but until then, I got a lot of high schools to check out, if you know what I mean. It's like I always say, if they are old enough to bleed then they are old enough to breed. Ha! Ha!

Later,

Dean

His face lit up. At least Dean got out. He did not know how far he would get, but at least he got out. He stared at the blade and wondered about the inscription written on the blade:

Hearst.

A thought raced through him, *There's a rich family with that name, that lives on the outskirts of town.*

"What the hell, it's worth a shot."

He grabbed his jacket with the knife in hand, and headed to the local antique and collectibles shop.

"Come right in, young fellow. How can I help you?" The pleasant store clerk smiled.

"Um, I got this knife see, someone close gave it to me."

"Let me take a look at it, hhm..." The store clerk put his glasses on to examine the blade more closely. "Oh my God! I can't believe it! Do you know what you've got here?"

He tried to hide his bewilderment, "Um, of course I do."

"This is the legendary switchblade of the Hearst family. Patty Hearst used to carry this around with her when she committed bank robberies!"

"You don't say? How much will you give me for it?"

"Oh...I don't know...It's most likely stolen."

"That doesn't really matter, does it?" he asked through a gritty sneer.

"Hey, you're that Billy kid, aren't you?"

Billy dashed a look around the store.

"Five hundred dollars." The clerk blurted.

He deciphered the greedy gleam in the store clerk's eye. There was no doubt in his mind that the clerk lusted for the blade.

"One thousand, no less," Billy retorted with confidence.

"I can call the cops and get it for free."

"I can run this knife right through your fucking skull."

They stared at each other for a few moments; the clerk decided to end the Mexican Stand-off.

"Okay, okay, you got it. Just sell it to me."

"You know what, I changed my mind. I like Patty Hearst.

I heard she has 'evil sex.'...two thousand."

"What? you got to be—"

"What?...psycho? No, I'm just, Billy."

The clerk sighed, "Alright kid, alright, two thousand dollars and not a penny more."

"There you see, it's not hard dealing with the Devil."

The clerk stroked the infamous blade, in awe. He then counted out the money and shoved the cash into Billy's waiting hand.

He stashed it and headed out with a big fat smile. As he rushed out of the store and headed back to the house, the clerk dialed 9-1-1.

"Hello, yeah, a punk-kid, greaser just robbed my store. Yeah, yeah, yeah, I can identify him...his name is Billy Bomm."

***

Around five o'clock in the evening Billy scrambled into the garage and pulled out his bike.

"Holy shit Jean, we are actually gonna do it! Ride off into the sunset with Savanna."

She did not respond. She did not have to because when he tried to kick start her, she didn't turn over.

"No, this is not happening, what are you doing, baby?" "Come on, come on, please! Please! ...Fuck!" he stopped pleading, and leaned on the bike, and lit a cigarette.

"Why are you doing this to me, Jean?"

"I'm sorry Billy, but this has gone too far. She does not love you. You are her scapegoat for the problems she faces. You will see it all later. Her true colors will shine and it will blind you."

"No, no Jean, you got it all wrong. She loves me and it's going to be just like my dream. So please, have some faith in me."

He tried again to start the obstinate motorcycle. She turned over, but something was wrong with her, the engine ran rough and sputtered. He didn't care right then, he gunned it, and headed to Savanna's house. He drove up on the lawn and parked in the middle of the yard. He strutted over to the front door and rang the door bell.

Her father opened the door.

"Yes, may I help you?" The old man eye-balled him hard.

"Yeah, I'm here for your daughter."

"Excuse me, *who* are you?"

"I'm fate, and I'm taking Savanna away from this so-called family."

She flew down the staircase carrying her luggage, and slipped past her dad and out the door.

"And where do you think you're going, Missy?" her flustered and dumfounded father asked.

"I'm sorry dad, I can't handle this anymore. The whole family keeps pushing Bradley on me. I just need to get away. I'll call you later."

She ran past Billy to Jean and hopped on the back of the customed bike.

Billy stood in defiance on the porch with Savanna's stunned father, his fists clenched.

Another stand-off ensued.

"Boo!" Billy blurted.

The startled old man jerked backwards.

"Well, nice meeting you sir, or should I call you, Dad?"

"I'm calling the police! You're not taking my daughter anywhere!"

He laughed as he strolled back to the bike and an anxious Savanna.

"I got twenty dollars. I don't know how long that is going to last though."

"Don't worry baby. I got more than enough for quite a while."

They ripped down the street. She held on tight.

Dusk crept in, a fiery glow covered part of the town. As they rolled closer to the raging fires, they could feel the intense heat. A huge house fire raged down the block. He knew who lived there. It belonged to the family of a close friend of The Bradster. They rode on, he thought, *Jimmy strikes again*. Further down the road, two patrol cars were positioned with their lights on and the doors wide open. The officers were chasing someone down the road. As he rolled passed the cops closing in on their quarry, he recognized their target, "Fuck! It's Jimmy!" He slowed down.

Jimmy had a look of 'help me' written all over his face.

What should he do? His friend needed help, but he and Savanna were suppose to start a new life together.

Savanna sat up, holding him tighter and whispered in his ear, "Speed up Billy, keep going."

He refocused on the road ahead, and gunned it. He watched Jimmy's expression of disappointment in the side-view mirror. Jimmy relented. Betrayed by his friend in favor of a split-tailed whore! He knew the chase was over. He sensed Billy's new determination. What was the use of running? Lt. Gip's cop car came roaring up fast. Gip slammed on the brakes, the patrol car skidded and fish-tailed off to the side of the road. He pulled himself out of the car, wearing a hospital robe. "Get on the ground!"

In a daze, Jimmy ignored the command and walked closer to Gip. "They killed my brother!"

The hammer on Gip's .45 clicked back. "I said, get on the fucking ground, greaser!"

Jimmy marched faster, closer, screaming, "They killed my brother!"

"So help me, God, I will shoot you where you stand, boy."

Jimmy kept coming.

The outline of a figure and a black pompadour slid into the driver's side of the cop car.

An intense and committed Gip squeezed the trigger, the patrol car's siren blared, the errant bullet streaked past. Gip whipped around to face headlights aimed right for him. The tires screeched and smoked as it barreled toward him. The impact swatted the lieutenant up into the air and catapulted him back over the top of the car. His hard head bounced on the pavement like a basketball.

The patrol car came to a halt next to Jimmy.

The passenger door flew open. "Get in!" Dean commanded. "Get in, damn it!" Jimmy shook off the cobwebs and fog, and dove into the car.

"They say, third times a charm!" Dean peered at Gip, with his head out the window. He floored it and they were off down the road.

A staggering bloodied Gip rapid-fired several shots at them. He fell back as blood gushed down his face. "I'll get you!" he screamed as he emptied the magazine and continued to dry fire his weapon.

Gip was shrinking in the mirror as they raced off.

"He looked a little mad. What the fuck happened? I leave town for a little while and all Hell breaks loose."

Jimmy had tears rolling down his face, "They killed Max."

"What? Who killed Max?"

"Fucking Bradley, and those fucks. I've been burning each and everyone of those fuckers' houses down!"

Dean shook his head in disbelief.

"Fucking Billy's gone!"

"Gone where?"

"I don't know. He had Savanna on his bike, and he just kept going. I saw his face, he was not there!"

"Oh shit! Guy was right. I only came back to pick something up. I can't leave now. Let's go to the park and regroup." Dean slammed his hands against the steering wheel. He pulled up into the park. Sick Boy, Hank, and Guy were sitting on the park table, laughing.

"Cool cop car, man!"

Dean pointed his finger at Sick Boy, "Shut the fuck up. We got problems! Billy's gone!"

"Whad'ya mean he's gone?" asked Hank.

"He took off with Savanna, and it looks like he's not coming back."

"Fucking, bitch! The rumble is tonight!" Sick Boy punched the air, and paced, kicking up dirt and dust.

This was not the Billy they knew. They were filled with rage and betrayal. They sat in silence for few moments.

Sick Boy jumped up, "Fuck him! The rumble is still happening! We don't need that pussy!"

"Whoa! Whoa! Whoa! He'll be back, and Sick Boy, he will make you eat those words," Hank cautioned.

Sick Boy walked around the table and yelled, "Billy's a big, sloppy pussy! What was that, Billy? The pussy? Do you have anything to say, *pussy*?" Sick Boy cuffed his hand around his ear, feigning an expected response out of nowhere. "You see? he's gone! We are going to have this rumble! With me...ME! Leading the—"

"Who said anything about you leading?" asked Hank. "Fighting in the rumble is one thing, but *you* leading The Click? Billy won't put up with that!"

"Like I said, where is he now? Do you really want a pussy to lead The Click? Besides, I'm twice the greaser he ever was...could ever be."

"I've known Billy my whole life and you better hope he doesn't come back." A disgusted Hank had heard enough.

"Well then, fuck you." Sick Boy pointed and gestured aggressively at Hank. "You gonna bail on the rumble too?"

"I'll be at the rumble, but I will have no part of you taking over The Click," he said as he walked away from the group.

Dean said, "Jimmy, let's get out of here."

A reluctant Jimmy scuffled over to Sick Boy.

"See? Jimmy knows I'm the real deal!"

"I'm sorry Dean, Billy left us, and if Sick Boy can bring me revenge for my brother, then I'm with him."

"Whatever...I don't like this, but I'll roll with it, I'll rumble with you, and then I'm out of this fucked-up town." Dean went back to the stolen police car and drove off.

Jimmy and Sick Boy looked at Guy who had not said a word.

"So, what up, Guy? You want some action? Are you with us?"

Guy sucked a long, deep drag off his cigarette, "That's what I need."

"Good, then let's get to The Lot, it's almost rumble time."

They stormed off united, into the darkness.

***

A vacated unsuccessful Wal-Mart® building had been recently razed off the property. So much for putting the town "on the map" as the Wal-Mart® executives predicted and promised. Billy had always thought it would be poetic justice having a rumble where a defunct Wal-Mart® once stood. Two lamp posts on opposite sides of The Lot laid on the ground, fallen from grace. A small fire smoldered in the middle of the sullied property.

On the far edges, old decaying cars lined the perimeter. A '49 Mercury, a '65 G.T.O were the most recognizable models. Four, perhaps five, local greaser gangs had assembled there, fifty to sixty gang members milled around, anticipating the battle.

Dean and Hank arrived, Sick Boy, Jimmy, and Guy were already there. They grouped together and marched down the hill. One of the gang members in the middle of the field exhorted, "The Click is here!" The crowd chanted, raising and clanging their chains and swinging their baseball bats.

Sick Boy reached out and shook hands with a couple of the roughnecks, "You boys ready to take this town?"

The mob erupted again.

Hank and Dean were rather dismayed by what they were seeing, hearing.

"Yeah! So, where's Billy?"

"Billy's scared and I'm taking over!" Sick Boy exclaimed.

The horde then quieted.

"It doesn't matter! We came here to fight against what we hate. Ain't I right! We'll take this town over!" Sick Boy stated with self-absorbed authority.

The gangs were gaining confidence and they began their bone-chilling chants again. They didn't care who led them. They just wanted to fight for what they believed in.

Guy went over to a rusted out '62 Caddie and dumped all his cocaine onto the hood of the car. With his razor blade, he cut up a single line that stretched across the hood of the car. He slammed his face down and snorted the whole line. "Ahhhhh!" He tilted his head back, and nodded as his eyes rolled and bugged.

Several pair of headlights crested the hilly roadway. Their adversaries had arrived. They stood tough and defiant. As they stared down the oncoming vehicles.

One by one, the vehicles drove onto The Lot.

Some greasers raised their bats and chains and taunted the drivers. The cars stopped on the opposite side of The Lot. Bradley was the first to get out. They all started to pile out of their vehicles and it looked like the greasers were out numbered.

Bradley stomped his way to the greasers and looked around. "Where's Billy?"

"No Billy! Tonight you dance with me." Sick Boy said as he stepped into Bradley's face.

"What? Whatever...after I take care of your crazy ass, I'll find him and take care of him, too."

The two gangs started to bait each other, clanging beer bottles together with bats creating a deafening echo. The sound of switch blades ejecting added to the chorus. Then through the crowd, Guy stumbled with a chain wrapped around his fist. He stumbled up to Bradley and swatted him in the face. Bradley dropped quickly as Guy jumped on top of him, wailing away.

A clash of greasers and preps erupted into a brutal scene of fighting. Before long there was blood everywhere, and the utter anarchy, Bradley never got in one punch. Guy sat on top of him, beating his face into a bloody pulp.

Some of Bradley's boys pushed through the ferocious crowd and attempted to help him out. One picked up a stray crowbar and swung it at the back of Guy's head. The sound of bone cracking, rang through the crowd, yet it did not phase Guy, sky-high on coke, he did not feel it. Blood streamed from his head and ran down his body as he continued to pound on Bradley. The crowbar slammed two more times into his skull, finally, he crumpled to the ground.

Guy's bloody body convulsed and white foam and blood poured from his mouth. Dean and Jimmy teamed up on a taller prep named Josh. Dean jumped on Josh's back holding him, while Jimmy punched him in the ribs. Dean let Josh go and he wilted to the ground holding his rib cage. Jimmy kicked him in the face while he was down and continued to stomp on him.

Meanwhile, Sick Boy was taking on two preps. The first one he kicked in the balls, and the boy dropped to his knee's. Sick Boy grabbed the back of his head and knee'd him square in the face, sending a few of his front teeth flying.

The other prep wanted nothing to do with the dirty fighter; he ran for his life. Sick Boy chased after him, tackling him to the hard ground. He grabbed the frightened boy by his hair and smashed his face into the concrete. The bloodied kid screamed in horror as Sick Boy leaned in and bit his ear off. Sick Boy stood up and spit the chunk of ear out and ran to confront Hank.

Licking the blood from his mouth he screamed, "Hey Hank! Me and you!" he had a crazed look in his eyes.

Hank punched out the prep he fought with and turned to face Sick Boy.

"What, are you fucking crazy? We're on the same side!"

"I never did like you and now that Billy's gone nobody else will talk back to me. This is my gang!" Sick Boy charged Hank, and tackled him to the ground.

They rolled around and Sick Boy got on top of his chest. Hank jerked upward and thrust his head into Sick Boy's ribcage, he tumbled back.

Hank sprang to his feet and grabbed Sick Boy in a headlock. The two boys continued to grapple each other.

For the most part, the greasers were destroying the preps. The preps had not anticipated or envisioned that the fighting would be so dirty and violent. This was not playtime for the greasers. This was for all the bullshit, all the pent-up aggression, and all the problems they felt that they had against society and its perceived unfair rules. They took it all out on the preps and there were casualties, serious ones, which would bring serious consequences.

The preps finally realized the gravity of the violence; they feared for their lives and ran off.

Sick Boy and Hank remained locked in battle. The lingering greasers circled around the two gladiators to witness the unspeakable brutality.

Dean noticed Guy laying on the cold concrete and ran to help him. Guy laid motionless in his own pool of blood. White foam oozed slowly from his mouth. Brain matter dripped from his skull and ears. Dean redirected his attention on the noisy crowd that had encircled Sick Boy, and Hank.

"Hey, they got Guy! He's dead!" Dean fought his way through the crowd, pushing and shoving the bodies aside. Sick Boy was on top of Hank, swinging away at him.

"Get the fuck off him!" Dean ordered, as he grabbed Sick Boy by the neck and threw him off.

Hank and Sick Boy huffed and gasped for breath.

"You see that shit?...Hank attacked me for no reason!" accused Sick Boy.

The pumped up, frenzied crowd gawked at Hank.

"Whoa! Motherfucker you attacked—"

"And now you and Dean are teaming up on me!"

Dean refuted Sick Boy's outrageous claim, "This has gone far enough! You ain't no Billy! And I ain't following you!"

Hank struggled to get to his feet, "Yeah, Sick Boy! You're fucking crazy, man!"

Dean grabbed an exhausted Hank and shoved him aside.

Sick Boy stared at them with wild, crazy eyes. "Last chance! You with me or not?"

Dean lifted up his hand and flipped him off, while he backed away, dragging Hank with him.

Sick Boy stroked his chin, smiled, and watched them fade through the crowd.

CHAPTER 9

"Let him go abroad to a distant country; let him go to some place where he is not known. Don't let him go to the Devil, where he is known." —*Samuel Johnson*

Succubi

The ride to the cabin was long, and he could not stop thinking about what would happen to Jimmy.

I'm going to be happy for the first time in my life. He thought.

They arrived at the sequestered, beautiful mountain retreat. The moon glistened off the lake reflecting the heavens. Paradise! The cabin over-looked the lake and it was peaceful and quiet. They opened the front door. It creaked, the interior smelled of old, musty wood.

Savanna turned to him and kissed him on the cheek. He hoisted her up, and carried her over the threshold, as if they were newly-weds. He gently laid her down on the couch and walked over to the fireplace.

"I'm going to the store, Billy. Give me some money for food and wine."

"How much you need?"

"How much you got?"

"I've got two thousand dollars," he said proudly, hoping

to impress her.

A look of disbelief came across her face, "You didn't steal that or anything?"

"Nope, totally legit, thank you very much," his smile widened.

"Okay. Give me a thousand."

"What? Get the fuck out of here!"

"No, I'm serious."

"Why do you need so much?"

She swayed seductively up to him, and whispered in his ear, "Baby, you're not going to support me and my needs?" she gave him a light kiss on the cheek.

"Hehe," he giggled as he held the money out to her.

She ripped it from his hands.

"While I'm gone, why don't you get some firewood from outside."

"Um? Okay! Where's the chainsaw?" he asked cautiously.

She walked to the closet and pulled out an axe. She gave it to him smiling, "Here you go Mr. Bunyan."

"That's fine, that's fine. You watch, I'm going to bring back the biggest tree in this forest," he grinned.

She sashayed out the front door, blowing him a kiss.
That did it, he *really* needed to cut down some redwoods, or lift a few trucks, now.

He opened the front door, a cold, brisk wind hit him in the face. Night had fallen and he walked back in the house to layer his clothes before going outside.

He hiked through the forest looking for a good tree to chop down.

"Ah haa!"

He spotted a good ten foot tree in the distance. He had never cut down a tree before, so he decided to play a little game to pass the time.

"Now if I can cut this tree down, Savanna will love me forever." He walked up to the tree. Suddenly, before he knew what happened, he found himself careening down the side of the hill. He did not notice the steep slope, trudging through the darkness. He tumbled and tumbled downward, unhurt but encased in forest muck.

"Fuck! Shit! Motherfucker! Cocksucker Asshole! Cunt!" He swore all the way to the bottom of the hill. He slowly looked up and stared at the same tree he was looking at before he fell. That so-called ten-foot tree was just the top of a forty-foot one. As he laid at the bottom of the hill, next to the gigantic trunk, he began to laugh at himself.

"Ha! I feel like a fucking fish out of water here. Well, if she's going to love me forever, I've got to cut this tree down."

He stood up and went to work. He slammed the axe into the massive trunk and chopped away. Time flies by when you're working hard, and Billy lost track of time. Some final chops with the axe and the tree gave way.

"Timber!"

A thunderous crash echoed through the thick forested hillside. He began to cut some small pieces of wood off the tree to bring back to the cabin. An eerie howl in the distance made him chop a little bit faster.

It was dark and cold. His vivid imagination suggested that this would be a good plot, and location for a B-rated horror movie. His mind wandered as he gazed up at the stars.

Life is a big movie isn't it? Because I know I'm in some fucked up love drama, horror flick. I wonder if I'm going to have that Hollywood ending?

He stopped chopping and brushed his clothes and hands off, "Done."

He trekked up the hill and back to the cabin, carrying a hefty load of firewood. He opened the door and announced, "Honey, I'm home!"

She sat quietly facing the empty fireplace.

"Um, Savanna? I'm here."

He waited patiently. Still, no response from her.

Suddenly, the brooding beauty demanded, "Where the hell were you?"

"I was getting firewood, like you asked. You should see

the tr—"

She exploded, "You've been gone for three hours! I've been freezing, sitting here all alone!"

"But I was looking for a good tree for us. I thought maybe—"

"Well, you thought wrong!" her tone was wicked.

He did not know what to say. He had just experienced a side of her he had never witnessed before, or maybe, just never noticed. He stood silently and looked around the room. He saw the supplies she bought at the store. Mostly personal things for her and her alone. A bottle of expensive, designer perfume, and a fur coat.

"Well, the fireplace isn't going to start itself!" She poured herself a glass of wine.

He shuffled slowly to the fireplace and dropped the wood into it. He threw some newspaper in with the firewood, then he took out the Lucky Strike Zippo and lit the paper. He sat in front of the fireplace, staring at the Zippo, and feeling like shit. The fire went out and he quickly tried to get it started again so she would not scream at him, or freeze. He started to doubt his dream. It really hurt him the way she yelled, and for what?...catering to her needs. It made no sense to him.

As he sat alone in front of the fireplace, he suddenly felt two arms wrap around him.

"I'm sorry, Billy. I was just cold and lonely, that's all."

He glared at her, and she stared back at him.

"I'm sorry."

Her deep blue eyes melted him. He shrugged and said, "Forget about it."

She beamed, "No! I want to make it up to you, because you've been so good to me. You're everything a girl could ask for."

He stuttered, "How are you going to make up for it?"

"Oh I have something in mind." She looked at him with dreamy bedroom eyes.

"Well...ah...I've got something in mind too."

"I bet you do, but I just want to be held tonight."

"That's cool, whatever you want," he would do, and put up with just about anything, just to get close to her.

They sat wrapped in an intimate embrace. He kissed her neck, and the edges of her delicate ears, ever so softly. He laid her down in front of the fireplace as they continued to kiss passionately. They were lost in the moment, then suddenly she sat up, "Wait, Billy! Stop it!"

"What's the matter?"

"I don't know. It just seems too soon. I don't want a relationship right now."

"Okay, I'm sorry."

Her new attitude surprised him.

"I just want a friend. Billy, please, hold me," she started to cry.

He had his head on her shoulder. He sighed deeply, "Don't worry girl, you're with me now."

The fire went out again, and she looked into the fireplace.

"Billy, why does the fire keep going out?"

"I don't know. I cut down the biggest tree in the fucking forest."

She giggled, "Silly, you have to cut up old logs not fresh trees, they don't burn." She looked up and kissed him on the lips. "You're so cute. Thank you anyway, sweetie."

She wreaked seduction as the pouty bombshell poured herself another glass of wine. She moved closer to him, and leaned in for a kiss. He hesitated. He was not sure what she wanted from him, but he gave in to his enchantment. They embraced again. That fated night, their unforgettable, impassioned, tender love-making burned and consumed all their youthful energy in front of a smoldering, dying fire.

***

A couple of weeks passed. Billy and Savanna were having the greatest time together, joking, teasing each other, and engaging in a few intimate conversations from time to timc. They swam whenever the mood struck them, and under the moonlight at night, he would row her around the lake in the small bass boat, upon where, they would contemplate the future, the heavens, and the stars.

One morning, he woke up to an intoxicating aroma. He rolled out of bed and went into the kitchen; there she stood, cooking.

"Good morning, sunshine," she delivered some hot tasty-looking food to the oak-planked table.

He wanted to admire the mouth-watering bacon, eggs and sausages on the sizzling plate. But then he remembered what Dean had told him; her delicate vegetarian palate.

"Um, I'd rather not eat meat, Savanna."

"Really, Billy? I'm impressed!"

"Yeah, going to try something new."

She quickly emptied the plate of delectable meats into the garbage can.

He secretly frowned.

"So what are we having then?"

"Soy latte, and rice cakes. Don't worry it's good," she assured him, and placed the bland concocted assortment down on the table.

Billy cringed a little as he glared at the rice cakes.

"Shit, I didn't know those things were edible. I've been putting my beer cans on them for years," he joked, mocking the cardboard-looking excuse, masquerading as 'food.'

"No silly! They're *not* coasters. It's a sunny day today, I thought we could go down to the lake and sit on the boardwalk."

He took a small bite of his rice cake and feigned a smile. He tossed the 'coaster' out the window when she wasn't looking.

After breakfast, he grabbed her hand and they frolicked down the steps to the long boardwalk, that led to the shoreline. The sun glistened off of the crystalized lake, and the polished water beckoned to them. They sat down and dipped their feet in the warm water. She turned to him and smiled.

Billy's eyes opened wide with amazement, "Deja' vü! This is it, Savanna! My dream! This is the spot that I dreamed about us...together!"

"Oh, how sweet, you had a dream about us, together."

They inched closer and started to kiss.

He felt complete bliss for the first time in his life. A ringing phone from the cabin interrupted the intimate moment. She sprang to her feet, "It's probably my dad. I should answer it this time."

He begrudgingly nodded approval, but he did not want the sweet moment to end.

She jogged back to the cabin to quell her father's worry.

He lied down on the boardwalk and sighed. He was happy, but he still felt an uneasy tug in the pit of his stomach.

An hour passed and she had not returned. He waited about twenty more minutes and then headed back to the cabin.

He opened the front door and saw her crying on the sofa. He went to comfort her.

"What's the matter? Did your dad yell at you?" he asked with sincerity.

"Billy...Billy...it was Bradley on the phone. My dad gave him the number."

"Oh," he replied, conflicted by anger and sadness.

"He said I should come back. That things will be different."

"What are you crying about, Savanna? You are with me now. Don't I make you happy?"

"Yeah, but, I kinda miss him."

"What? What the fuck can you possibly miss about him? The abuse, or is it the disrespect?"

She looked down at the wooden floor, "I miss his closeness. I can't even remember the bad about him, only the good."

"Where does that leave us, Savanna?" he asked in a soft voice.

"Billy, I love you, but I'm not *in love* with you. I wish it could be, but I'm not."

"I love you so much, Savanna. Please, what can I do to make you happy with me?"

"You can just be my friend," she replicd

He looked into her eyes, a tear rolled down his face, "That's not fair to me, I have feelings for you that I've never felt before. Am I suppose to hide them and act like your friend?"

"Just..." she paused, and then hid her head between her legs.

Her words shocked and dismayed him. *One God damn phone call, and she's right back where she started.* The weeks with him meant nothing to her. He turned away. He couldn't bear to look at her. He stood up and stormed out the front door.

"Where are you going?"

"I don't know. I just need some time to think."

"I'm sorry, Billy."

"Yeah *sure* you are," he slammed the door behind him.

He pounced on his bike and started to ride, hard. He found a dirt path that led to a little shaded area. He laid down across the bike's leather seat and lit up a cigarette.

Billy, I told you. She does not love you. But you just had to learn the hard way.

He said nothing, and just took another drag off his cigarette.

She is just using you to escape her problems.

"Fuck Jean! What am I suppose to do? I love her. I just can't walk away from the girl that I love."

You must love yourself first, before you can love another.

"I don't know! I just don't know what to do anymore. She's all I got left."

You still have me.

"I know, but some things you just can't do for me. You know?"

No, I don't know. It never used to be like this. It was always you and me, against the world.

He did not reply because he knew she was right.

You missed the rumble. The whole town is probably in total turmoil, created by you. And you're missing it, to be with a chick. The old you would have been right in the middle of the Hell.

"I don't have it in me anymore. I've lost me!"

He slept restlessly on his bike that night occasionally waking up and staring up at the moon and stars knowing that no one felt like he did; that night, on the whole planet, possibly the universe.

A few more hours passed, and he woke up for good in a cold sweat, feeling void. He started his bike and rode back to the cabin to apologize. What for? He did not know, he just did not want to lose her. Faster and faster he rode trying to ease the pain that engulfed him.

Don't go running back to her! You two do not belong together. There is no use in trying to rescue someone that does NOT want to be saved!

"But she is drowning, Jean! I can make it still work, some how! I know deep down she has a heart for me."

He arrived at the cabin and flung the front door wide open.

"Savanna! Savanna! I'm sorry! Please, let's just talk!"

No response came, but he saw a letter on the kitchen table. He unwillingly approached it and read:

To my darling Billy,

This is hard for me to tell you, but I'm going back. I enjoyed every minute with you and I'll never forget it. But I love Bradley. I realized that when he called me. He said he was going to change for me. I'm sorry, but you're a great guy, I'm sure you will find someone special who will treat you right. Bradley and I are moving out of town, so I probably will never see you again. Please don't hate me, Billy. You always said you wanted to see me happy, well I am. I will always love you as a friend, and something a little more. I only wish things could be different between us. But that can never be. I'll miss you, and remember we will always have that special night, by the fireplace.

Love Savanna,

P.S. Cheer up, Buttercup

His heart sank. He felt as if he had aged many years right in that moment. He sat down and the tears began to roll as he lit a cigarette. What could he do? He had nothing left. No family, no place to live, no girl, and he ditched his friends when they needed him the most. He could not go back. He put his head back on the couch and shut his eyes. Images of Savanna, beautiful, uncaring Savanna ran through his head. It was not long before severe depression kicked in. He just sat there with no motivation, staring at the ceiling. The phone rang and rang, but he was in his own little comatose world as he lied on the couch. His conscious mind ignored the telephone, the world.

Another day passed, and there was no improvement in his mood. Still lying in the same position, he kept thinking, *I need her. She taught me how to love. She can't leave me now*. Over and over questions of *why this...now?...why?* exploded in his head. He had been in many fights and experienced other bad events in his life and always walked away without a scratch, but this time he was emotionally scarred. He put his head down and the tears flowed down his sad, pathetic, pale, cheeks.

The pounding on the door did not phase him. He lied motionless on the couch, dead to the world.

"Billy! I know you're in there, it's me, Pike!"

He wiped the tears away, stumbled to the front door, and slowly opened it.

"What the hell? What are you doing here, and how did you find me?"

"It wasn't hard, dude. I see and hear lots of things because nobody pays attention to a little kid like me. I overheard Savanna talking or should I say fighting with Bradley inside the park. She said you were up here and she told Bradley to leave you alone because you are not worth it."

"Fucking, two-faced, bitch!"

"Anyway, that is not why I am here. Shit is going down! The Click won the rumble, Sick Boy took control of The Click and he has plans for you. He's been telling everybody that you are weak, and a pussy for ditching your friends. Your friends, your gang, The Click...they are now your enemies."

Billy lit up another cigarette and looked around in disbelief. He noticed a small red light flashing at the end of the table. He stood up and dragged his feet over closer to identify the blinking beacon. A message waited for him on the answering machine. It was left over an hour ago. *That's weird...I was here. Maybe it's Savanna.* He pressed the button and the message played:

"Hey, you little, prick. Bradley here, or the Bradster, what ever you prefer. I'd rather be called winner because I might have lost the battle, but I've won the war. I didn't care about that stupid little rumble. I got Savanna and we both know that she is the real trophy. She's jumping on my dick as I speak."

In the background he could hear her coo, "Bradley, put down the phone and come to bed."

"Anyway, duty calls. Just wanted to let you know that you lost, Billy boy, and between me and you, not to worry, I'll fuck her really good, in your honor. See you in Hell."

He became so angry he picked up the phone receiver, forgetting it was just a message and yelled, "Not if I see you first!" He then shoveled up the base of the phone and threw it across the room, smashing it into little pieces. He slammed his hands on the counter and stared at the floor. Breathing heavily, eyes wide, and ablaze, he chanted as if in ritual, "Never! Never!" He snapped to, and his trademarked shit-grin crossed his face, "Never again!" He laughed hard, as though he suffered from insanity.

"What are you going to do?" Pike tried to hide his trembling hands.

Fire filled his eyes, "EVERYTHING!" He ran through the front door breaking the hinges free from the door jamb. He straddled Jean and kick-started her in one fluid motion. He then tore down the road, determined for revenge, and vindication.

I know what you're thinking, and I like it. There is no stopping you now baby, it's you and me forever.

He reached in his pocket and threw the Zippo into the lake, as he rode by the shoreline.

"It's pay back time Jean! To everyone that has ever treated me like shit. To society, that backed me in this corner! I'm busting out! Old Billy is back and he's got nothing to lose. I'm gonna show those people the gates of Hell. I lived there for so long, I think it's time to invite all of them to where I live and breathe!"

"AAAAAA-HAAAAAH!" he yelled, as he ripped down the road. His internal fire and gritty resolve were back, more than ever. No more 'a rebel without a cause.' His reasons were plentiful, and the town had no idea what was about to hit them. A genuine Billy bomb!

CHAPTER 10

"...and I looked, and behold a pale horse and it's rider, his name that sat on him was Death and Hell followed with him."
—The Holy Bible, Revelations, Chapter 6, verse 8

Vindication

The rumble was over. The Click had left the town in ruins. Sick Boy claimed the leadership, and not a single person stood up against him. He called a meeting at the park to discuss what would happen next.

"Yeah!" Shouted Sick Boy as he watched Jimmy show up.

"Hey, Sick Boy! How's it hanging?" Jimmy asked with a nod.

"Hanging to the left today," he snickered.

"What is this meeting about?"

"Just wait till everyone shows up, I want to talk about something."

Hank and Dean approached from the wooded area to the north.

"Hey! There you fuckers are!" Sick Boy yelled.

"What do you want Sick Boy?" Hank still distrusted him after their last encounter. Dean didn't say anything, he kept quiet, smoking a cigarette.

"I brang you all here because we are all that is left of The Click. The four of us."

"Cut the small talk, what are you getting at?" Hank was in no mood, or impressed by his antics.

"I don't know about you, but Billy abandoned us for a chick, and in my book that's not cool, or respectable. He lost his fire and I'm just beginning." Sick Boy raised a fist in the air, shaking it proudly.

"You know Sick Boy, I really don't care that your filling in for Billy while he's gone; but to take over, I don't know," Hank shook his head in staunch disapproval.

"Fuck Billy! He's a pussy! I knew this the first day I met him. I'm the one who won the rumble and took back this town for the greasers. He could never do that."

"Yeah! He's right. Fuck Billy! It's because of him, my brother is dead."

"See, Jimmy is with me!"

"Billy started this Click for kids like us; who came from broken homes, that have no family or future. Kids who think fighting and wrenching on hotrods and bikes is a better use of time than watching M.T.V. and football. What you are trying to do, I want no part of. I know I'm trash and I will never amount to anything else but trash. The one thing I value is friendship, and Billy, as stupid, or crazy as he is, he will always be my friend. Billy brought you into The Click because he saw potential in you, not to backstab him. I've known him for a long time now and I have two words for you. Watch out!" Hank pointed his finger at Sick Boy and walked away.

"Fuck you too, then! I don't need your loser ass anyways," Sick Boy sneered at Dean and waited for his response.

"I don't know what to tell you, 'Sick Boy,' but, I've never liked you. I've seen too many of the so-called A.K.A.'s from the inside, and they go nowhere. My loyalty remains with Billy."

Sick Boy did not care for his mocking tone and marched up into Dean's face, "You have a big mouth for a pretty boy. Maybe I should change that for you," he pulled out a box cutter and swiped it across Dean's face. He yelled, "Fuck you! Who do you think the Greasers are going to follow? The one who won them the rumble or a pussy who ran off with some bitch?"

Dean stumbled back and wiped his face. He stared at the blood on his hand. He became angry and started for Sick Boy, but Jimmy jumped in between them, holding Dean back.

Dean pushed Jimmy off. “What the fuck is wrong with you, Jimmy? You gonna stick with this cocksucker?”

Jimmy kept silent.

Dean backed away and stormed off after Hank.

Sick Boy said, “We don’t need them, we don’t need The Click. We got a town full of greasers. We will start up a new gang. From now on we are known as, The Firecats,” he stood proudly.

“*That* name sucks,” Jimmy quietly said under his breath.

“What? What did you just say?”

Jimmy hung his head low, “I didn’t say anything.”

***

Billy rolled into town and the place looked different, like an aged dreamscape. He rode past his old house and discovered new yellow police tape had been secured to it and all along the front yard.

He assumed the cops placed it there after they found Max’s body. He did not see anyone hanging out at the usual local places. He passed the park and still saw no one.

“What the fuck happened to this town. What did I do?”

It’s not your fault, it’s society! We did not ask for it, but we got it. We just have other ideas on how things should be.

“Yeah, maybe your right. And what is this ‘we’ stuff?”

Face it Billy, I am the only thing you got left in this world. Now it’s time to listen to me!

He gripped her handlebars tighter and asked, “What do you have in mind?”

You were born with a purpose. I never knew what it is, until now. Look at the power you have, because of you, this town will never be the same. This town is only the beginning. Who knows what we are capable of accomplishing.

Jean continued to feed him poisonous thoughts as he burned down the road at treacherous speeds.

Darkness fell and he stopped by the store where he sold the knife.

"Hey there, young fellow! How are you doing?" asked the nervous clerk.

He approached the man with an intense stare, "I never got your name."

"It's Roy, like the sign says outside."

Billy glanced back at the door sign.

"Roy, I need my knife back."

"Sorry son, a deal is a deal."

He did not really listen to what the man said, "I need, my knife, back," he growled.

The uneased clerk stood, staring into space.

"GIVE ME THE FUCKING KNIFE!"

"I don't want any trouble, boy," Roy pulled out a double barrel shotgun and pointed it at Billy's head.

He looked up at the shotgun and stared straight into the barrel. He smiled and within a split second, he swiped the gun out of the clerk's hands.

He pointed the gun steadily at Roy's face, "You know you shouldn't play with guns, someone always winds up getting hurt."

"NO! Please! Don't kill me I have a wife and kids!" Roy stammered and pleaded as he got on his hands and knees.

He remained silent for a torturous moment, "Just because you have a wife and kids means I should let you live? What the fuck you trying to say, asshole? I have no wife, nor kids! Should I die then? You saying you're better than me?" he shoved the gun hard against the clerk's forehead.

"NO! NO! I mean, have pity on me, please," Roy sobbed loudly.

He took a few steps back and looked around. "You have it all, don't you? Your own shop! Wife and kids! Probably a nice house! The whole nine yards!" He began to knock merchandise off of the shelves and displays, making a wreck out of the whole store.

"I got nothing! But I can take that all away from you! A

bastard kid! A mourning widow! A house burnt to the ground! Then you will have nothing! They will all have nothing!"

Just then he spotted the knife in a glass display case. He ran to the case and smashed the glass with the butt of the shotgun. He grabbed the knife, and as he headed out the door he picked up a gasoline can. He suddenly turned around and leered at the cowering clerk. "Now listen to me Roy!" He whipped up the shotgun and squeezed the trigger. The buckshot struck the cowering clerk in the head. Blood, hair, skull, and brain matter flew all over the back wall.

"All good things must come to an end!" He stared at the lifeless body, crouched down, and started to dig through Roy's pants. He pulled out the man's wallet, and grabbed the dead man's family photo. He stared at the young boy in the picture. "Welcome to my world kid." He then defiantly stomped outside, filled up the gasoline can, cradled it across the front of Jean's seat and rode off into the night, looking for trouble.

He rode fast, hard, and reckless. Headlights appeared in the distance. The car went past him and then the driver slammed on the brakes. He twisted his head around, but he couldn't tell who it was. He jammed down hard on the bike's brakes and skidded out of control, coming to a shaky stop in the middle of the road. *Looks like somebody wants to get hurt.* He kicked the stand down and walked to the car with clenched fists.

"Get out of the car! Come on you cunt! Let's see what you got!"

"Billy? Is that you?"

Hank and Dean jumped out of the car. Hank embraced his friend.

"Holy shit, Billy! Where have you been?"

Billy pushed Hank back and stared at both of them, "Friend or foe?" Anger filled his raw, bloodshot eyes.

"Billy it's us, Hank and Dean."

He believed that they were sincere and loyal. He relaxed his posture, "What happened to your face, Dean?"

"Fuck, Billy! Sick Boy, he took over The Click. All the Greasers are going to unite under him! Guy is dead. The town is a war zone! I'm sorry, but this is some heavy shit. I'm a lover, not a fighter, I'm too pretty for this shit," Dean said.

A relieved Hank said, "I knew you would come back, buddy."

Billy lit a cigarette, "Guy is dead?" he shook his head in reverence to his fallen friend.

"What are we gonna do?" asked Hank.

"Finish it," Dean's eyes told Billy that he wanted no part of the war. "Well Dean, it's been real. I'll catch you in the next life."

"It's not over Billy, there's always other towns and other high schools with little hot girls," Dean ranted.

"I'm not running from nobody, not Bradley, not Sick Boy, nobody!"

"You lost yourself, Billy!"

"No, that is where you are wrong, Dean. I *found* myself."

Billy threw down his cigarette with complete confidence, he went back to his motorcycle.

Dean nodded his head, he understood and scuffled away, fearful of the mayhem to come. He jumped in the car and rode off into the night, they would never see him again.

They watched as Dean drove away, "You always find out who your real friends are when the shit hits the fan."

He followed Billy to his motorcycle and asked, "So what's the plan?"

"Sorry Hank, this is my calling not yours. I might not come back. It's time to start chasing your own tail," he fired up the bike.

Hank inferred, *It's Billy's way of saying goodbye.*

"I understand. Well, brother, we been through a lot together. Go show them some Hell."

Billy revved up the bike and stoked his own internal fire, "Will do!" he then screamed on down the road.

He again rode fast, and hard, not caring about a damn thing. Images of hate filled his mind; his father, Bradley, Sick Boy. The angrier he became, the faster he burned down the road.

Suddenly, something hit him on the temple, and he went

down. He slid on the gravel road, finally coming to a stop a couple of hundred feet down the road.

He slowly stood up, groggy and dazed, he reached for his head and felt the blood gushing out. He heard crazy laughter in the distance. Billy refocused his eyes, there Jimmy stood proud in the middle of the road, a rock tightly gripped in his hand.

"Not a bad plan there, Billy. It worked once before!" Jimmy screamed.

"Jimmy! What the fuck are you doing?"

"What am I doing? What the fuck are you doing? This is not your turf anymore. It's Sick Boy's."

"Is that a fact? I'm the one who broke you out, gave you a place to live and let you join my crew. This is how I get repaid?"

"You broke me out only to put me in your Hell. Fuck you Billy! My brother died because of you. You left me to be caught by those fucking pigs. You're done!"

"Things got out of hand. Shit happens, and I'm sorry about Max."

"Yeah, I'm sorry too. Sorry for what I have to do," Jimmy stomped toward him with the rock, itching to be thrown.

"If you play with fire, you get burned," warned Billy. He grabbed his lighter and lit another cigarette. He noticed that his gas can had spilled out on the road, a small pool of high-test fuel collected by the prone spout. Jimmy walked right into the puddle.

He flicked the cigarette, it bounced off of Jimmy's chest and fell into the pool of gasoline. An explosion of flames wrapped around Jimmy's entire body. He screamed in agony.

Billy watched him burn...*What a fitting end to a pyro.*"

He limped back to his bike and picked it up off the ground. He tried to start her, but she would not kick over. "Come on baby! One more time for me." With a loud roar, the engine came to life.

"You okay, Jean?"

Yeah, babe. Just some minor scratches.

He ripped down the road, heading for the park. He needed to find Sick Boy, and right the wrong.

On the way, he passed The Hills. He took a sharp left turn and rode to Savanna's house. He had some things he wanted to get off his chest. He pulled up to her house and revved the engine. He spotted Bradley's car parked out front. He smiled because he contemplated engaging in some self-entertainment at Bradley's expense. The curtains slid apart, two shadowy figures appeared through the window. A few seconds later, the front door swung violently open.

"Listen to me you little prick. I'm gonna call the cops if you don't get the hell out of here!" Savanna's father yelled furiously.

Bradley came rushing out through the door with a golf club in hand, "Call the cops, Dad! I'll hold him here!"

Her father bolted back into the house to place the 9-1-1 call.

He leaned on his bike, smoking a cigarette, paying no attention to the blood gushing down his face.

"Billy!" Savanna ran out of the house.

"Get back in the house, bitch!" Bradley ordered.

Billy's anger intensified.

"Oh, I've been waiting for this moment for a long while. Nowhere to run this time, Billy boy!"

He looked at Savanna, she waited docile on the door steps.

"What are you looking at? She doesn't want you. She's mine!"

"I came to say goodbye to her. I know that she can never love a guy like me."

"Oh, how *sweet*! —Over her dead pussy!"

He stomped up to the doorstep and Bradley rushed him. He side-stepped him, stuck out his foot, and sent Bradley tripping and stumbling.

Billy's piercing eyes stabbed at Savanna. He then took off on Bradley, repeatedly kicking him in the stomach, while She watched in horror. He picked up the golf club and cracked Bradley in the back of the head, knocking him unconscious. He then grabbed the limp boy by the collar, and dragged him to the doorstep and dropped him at her feet. He looked at her and smiled, "This piece of shit right here, is what you love?"

She choked on her words through the tears that streamed down her face, "Yes, please don't hurt him anymore, Billy!"

Expressionless, without emotion, he propped Bradley's head up on the side of the first concrete step. He stomped down with all his might onto the back of the boy's skull. Bradley's head crackled and split open, his body writhed, contorted, and twisted. He had breathed his last. His lifeless body finally stopped quivering.

She dropped down to her knees beside her fallen beau, "AHHHH NOOOO!! I love him!"

"Yeah? Well, I loved you!" He turned away from her cowering body and walked back to his bike.

Savanna's wailing faded.

He started his bike and rode off. He looked back in his side-view mirror and watched her hold Bradley's spent body in her arms.

"Look at that, Jean. Even after death, she still embraces him with love. I couldn't be so lucky."

The fuck with her! She will never have true love because she sees with a blind eye. Let her wallow in her useless pain.

"Yeah! You're right, Jean. You're always right."

Finally arriving at the park, he saw a great gathering of old hotrods, motorcycles, and muscle cars. A big bonfire lit the entire park. Surrounding the fire stood a group of roughneck greasers. He positioned Jean at the crest of the hill, overlooking the park and sauntered down the hill to the raging fire. He yelled, "Sick Boy!...Sick Boy!"

Brimming with confidence, Sick Boy strutted and emerged from out of the crowd, "Well, so the king has come back to reclaim his throne. Well tough shit! The Firecats are mine!"

The hoodlums cheered him on.

Billy scoffed at all of them. *Fools!* "Firecats? What kind of pussy name is that? This is my Click!"

Sick Boy stepped into his face, "Not any more!"

Billy searched the angry faces in the crowd, it seemed to

him that they were nothing more than a bunch of lost souls who would go with the flow, and follow the herd like blind, mindless, sheep being led to the slaughterhouse. *...Fucking posers*! *...Half of these guys were just jocks and preps a few weeks ago, now look at them. It makes me want to puke.* His fierce eyes pierced Sick Boy, "You want this? You have to earn it. I'll give you a shot. If you can knock me down just once, I will walk away. You can have The Click or the Firecats, whatever you're calling them, and I will leave town."

Sick Boy replied in mid-thought, "Just an ol' fashion fist fight, huh?

"You're not afraid of me, *are you*?" he mocked.

"I ain't afraid of nothing. Nothing!" he yelled while he strutted, showing off for the blood-thirsty spectators.

Billy walked under one of the lamp posts and Sick Boy went to the other. A big circle of greasers surrounded them to watch what they thought would be the 'the fight of the century.'

A crack of lightning set the stage and thunder roared through the thick atmosphere. The rain poured down, and doused the light from the fire, smoke billowed into the glum sky.

The enraged boys stood there, glaring at each other. Red-tinted water dripped from Billy's face. He gave Sick Boy his shit-grin, egging him to bring it on. Sick Boy screamed and charged him.

He stood his ground, he did not budge, he waited for his attacker.

Sick Boy leaned his stampeding body forward, aiming for his sworn enemy.

Billy side-stepped and cranked out a blistering right hook. He shuffled aside and then pumped a straight left jab smashing Sick Boy's throat, he collapsed to his knees unable to breathe. He looked up at Billy, Sick Boy strugged for breath, holding his throat with both hands. Blood leaked through his fingers. As his hands dropped limp to his sides, the spectators gasped at the sight of the switchblade buried deep into his crushed windpipe.

"And now you know, *Sick Boy*, now everyone knows why

you could never become a leader. You follow some of the rules. This isn't a stinkin' game. Now, sit there, and bleed, that's all you're good for!"

The crowd of shocked boys stood in silence as they watched Sick Boy gurgle on his own blood.

"Who else? Any of you? You want to be like me?" he bellowed at the quieted mob.

They all remained silent, stunned.

He drifted back to his bike. The crowd, like the parting of the sea, cleared the way for him. He straddled Jean and roared off. He sped along heading for Dead Man's Curve. Riding the winding and twisting road helped him think, and clear his head.

Headlights on high beam lit up the roadway from behind. Then flashing red and blue lights stroked through the darkness, the siren pierced the rumbling thunder. The lights and the wail of the siren caused a trance-like state to come over him; it shrouded him in vicious flashbacks of his slain mother. He shook his head, releasing the grip of the horrible memory.

Gip, and O'Neil were hard after him. Through Dead Man's Curve they gave wild chase.

Billy twisted back on the throttle, accelerating.

"You're not getting away from me!" Gip yelled out the window.

"Yes! Gimp, come join the party!" he throttled harder.

Where are we going, Billy?

"To the unknown." Tears rolled down his face. "Fuck Savanna! Fuck The Click! Fuck those stinkin' pigs, and fuck this fucked-up world!" Jean's tach redlined to the limit; the strained bike burned down the road at over one-hundred-twenty miles per hour.

The road is about to end soon, there will be no turning back.

Faster and faster he flew, up the dead-end road to destiny.

"What's he doing?" asked O'Neil.

"He's ending it all! Fucking psycho kid!" Gip tried to catch up to the determined boy.

Faster, up the hill, the bike climbed. The lights of the

whole town sparkled below. 125...130 miles per hour. Billy cocked back his fist, and punched the speedometer as he jettisoned off the cliff into the cold night air.

"Never again!" he shouted as Jean's red taillight faded off into the darkness.

Gip and O'Neil screeched to a halt on the edge of the cliff and burst out of their car. They stared into the empty darkness and could only hear a soft breeze whistling through the crisp night air.

"Good riddance to the little asshole puke," the lieutenant goobered a ball of spit over the cliff's edge and limped back to the car, "Come on, O'Neil...You coming or what? We got a lot of paper work to do."

O'Neil stood on the edge of the cliff staring through the blackness and down on the town lights for what seemed to be an eternity to Gip.

"Come on, god-damn-it!" Gipp growled. "The punk is dead!"

O'Neil stuffed his hands into his pockets and slowly shuffled his way back to the car.

Epilogue

The morning sun brought the police forensic team, and the coroner out to the sight. A sub-contracted cleaning company waited patiently to get the okay to clean up the debris littering the bottom of the canyon.

Although the team of detectives and cadaver dogs scoured the canyon walls, crevices, and floor, all they found was the burned out shattered frame of Billy's motorcycle. The charred speedometer read 138.

He had achieved his *Lion's Share*. It wasn't about a girl or society, or respect. It was about living fast and dying hard, and young in a turbulent world where he lived as a 'king.'

His body was never found. Rumors consumed the town's folk that he had survived the crash and drifted off into the black of night to witness another sunrise, and more. Others said that he was such a badass, that the Earth opened up and Hell swallowed him, whole.

My sister Angel, always told me, "never, ever, be like Billy," I must admit, I looked up to him. To me, a snot-nosed, gangly and awkward kid; he was a god. I did take his advise about music though. The guitar he gave me? I practiced relentlessly with an intensity I cannot begin to describe to you. I started a successful band and crafted a new style of music. I dedicated this new brand of music to Billy because I'll never forget. He lived in our world but perceived a different existence and meaning, and lived by it. I suppose some would say he was crazy, perhaps deviant. Some would even call him 'psycho,' so, that jacket stuck. Just like he did, we play fast, we play hard, we are the new breed of 'Hell On Wheels.'

...We are...*Psychobilly*.

May you rest in peace, Billy.

Breinigsville, PA USA
16 September 2009

224241BV00002B/4/A

9 781893 660151